OUR LITTLE SECRETS

D. M. BROCKINGTON

SOUTHERN GIRL MEDIA

This book is for every woman who's ever reclaimed her sexiness.

RIDING THE WAVE

1

I call it "riding the wave". What else could you possibly call it? You can't stop it once it gets started, so you may as well go with the flow with as little resistance as possible. I'm now able to recognize the signs. If I'm in public, I know I've got about thirty seconds to a minute to either get out of there, or brace myself and try not to show what is happening. It starts with a tingling, and then I get warm and flush. As the heat begins to build up, I often find myself throbbing with an ache that is usually best relieved in the presence of a lover. But I don't have a lover. And if I did, he certainly couldn't be with me 24/7. So I cross my legs and breathe deeply. At that point, there is nothing left to do but ride it out. If I try to fight it, it just becomes more intense, thus making the entire scene that much more embarrassing. If I ride the wave, then it's over as quickly as it started.

I told my doctor about the orgasms soon after they started up again. I was concerned that there was something seriously wrong. There wasn't. No tumor. No seizures. No hormone imbalance. No blood poisoning. Dr. Acetta, my ob/gyn, sat me down with a very serious look on his face when he delivered the test results. He gave me the "I've known you for years, you are one of my favorite patients" speech. I was waiting for the diagnosis so that we could get to the cure.

"Stephanie, I have to tell you that after all of that testing, we didn't find any physical cause for your condition. I staffed your case with my colleagues here in the practice, and we unanimously agreed that I should make a referral to a psychologist for you."

"A referral? As in a shrink. Because since you can't find anything wrong physically, it has to be all in my head?" I started to feel panicky.

"I'm saying that there may be causes that are not physical. I have made a referral to a great psychologist. Her name is Dr. Lisa Hamilton. She's very good at what she does. She primarily works with women who have experienced trauma, but she's really interested in your case."

"I see. Well, let me think about it."

"Don't think too long, Stephanie. The longer you take, the worse things may get."

And now, I'm pulling into the parking lot outside of Dr. Hamilton's office. Again. She ended the last session by giving me homework: to make a list of all the things that I'm anxious about. I thought it was a dumb idea. That's what I was there to talk with her about. So, I didn't do it. No big deal really. I'm paying her...

Oh shit. Oh. Damn!

I am just putting the Jeep in park when it starts. I squeeze the steering wheel with both hands because there isn't much else for me to do. Until a couple of months ago, I didn't know that 30 seconds could be so long. The sigh that escapes is mixed with pleasure and annoyance. Why can't this happen when I'm in the Jacuzzi with some jazz playing in the background, or in bed after a busy day or, hell, even in the shower first thing in the morning? Nope, here I am in a parking lot. I have really got to get this under control. This one happens to be pleasurable, not painful. I really want to give in to it, but I never lose sight of the fact that I am in my car, although that doesn't stop me moaning and trying to refrain from putting my hands between my legs.

It takes a minute before my breathing returns to normal. I finally step out of the Jeep and slam the door. I do a thorough clothes check and adjustment before heading toward the office building. And that is when I notice the man standing on the steps smoking a cigarette.

The man grins and moves to the side to let me pass. "I could have helped you out with that," he sneers. I don't even speak as I charge past him and grab the door. That's what I get for driving the Jeep without the top on.

2

———

Dr. Lisa Hamilton is supposedly best suited to help me deal with my condition, and is so not my image of a psychiatrist. They're paid best friends who listen to all your trouble, ask you how you feel about everything, and look like retired school teachers. Nothing shocks or phases them. Not so with Dr. H. She's a forty-something blonde with a pixie haircut. Not your old school Southern Belle. She's more like Athletic Barbie- tall, lithe, and very tan. Not that spray on mess either. You can tell it's the real deal because her skin is a little wrinkly around her neck. I like it. Her office has pictures of her on a boat holding up fish of various sizes, that I presume she has actually caught. She keeps a pair of running shoes near the door, and has a model kayak on her desk. I have a pretty good idea of how she manages her own mental health.

As I settle into the overstuffed leather chair that lets out a "pufft" as I sit down, Dr. Hamilton looks me over.

"Hey Stephanie, how ya' doin'?"

"I'm good. Sort of."

"I just watched you have an episode in the Jeep. What was that about?"

Did I mention that Dr. H seldom wastes words? Cutting to the chase is her trademark. Two of the walls of her office are floor-to-ceiling windows. Basically, she has a great view of the parking lot and the marsh behind it. Of course she saw me.

"Just riding the wave. It's the first one I've had in a two days."

"What were you thinking about right before that happened?"

I rub my hands along the arms of the chair. The cool leather begins to warm up under the friction from my palms. "I was thinking about the fact that I didn't do my homework assignment. You know, the list of my anxieties."

"Why not?"

At first, I'm slow to answer, but then I decided to jump right in with the excuses. "This was my last week at the office. I had several good-bye lunches from different departments. I had to clean out my office, and I got the keys to the store from the realtor. And last weekend I went to Charlotte to hang out with Rachel. Things have been so busy. It just didn't make the cut on the To Do list."

"I see. So why do you think you had an episode in the car?"

"Probably because I didn't do something that I was tasked to do. The goody-two-shoes in me had a problem with that."

"Do you always do what people ask of you?"

"Actually, no. I've never really been a people pleaser. I don't see the benefit in it."

"That's certainly an interesting response. Why is there no benefit in doing what someone asks of you?"

"I'm not saying that I NEVER do things at the request of others, but I have found that when my initial reaction is no, and I say yes anyway, I'm extremely miserable. I have watched a lot of women make themselves very unhappy and unnecessarily busy because they refuse to say no. Folks either like you or they don't, and it's seldom because of what you do for them." My words rush out in a flurry of heat.

A flash of surprise danced across her face, and then was quickly gone. She jotted down a few words on the pad on her desk, and then resumed her clinical posture.

"Do you think you would have benefitted from making a list of your anxieties?"

"I'm sure I would have. It was just a busy week is all." Why am I starting to feel and act like a petulant teenager? I am here to get help. Dr. H. remained unfazed.

"Let's do it now. You can make a list of all of your anxieties during this session." Before I could answer, she reached into her draw and pulled out a legal pad. She then grabbed a pen out of a red mug with the word "Diva" on it in bold black script, and slid the pen and paper across the desk to me.

I reached over and took the items and placed them on my lap. I looked out of the window behind Dr. Hamilton at the grasses growing out of the marsh. They were swaying in the gentle breeze. Apparently the consequence of not doing homework at home is doing homework in session. I looked back down at the blank pad and began to write:

Opening a bookstore in this economy?

Did I do the right thing by letting my daughter go live with her dad?

Will my store make money?

Will I be able to pay my bills?

Will I be able to retire?

Is the bookstore a whim or a passion?

Will I regret leaving corporate America?

Will my mother stop trying to find me a husband?

When I was done. I slid the pad back across the desk. Dr. H read in silence, and then asked: "Why did you leave off your orgasms?"

"What?"

"You didn't list your orgasms as part of your anxiety. Why?"

I blink a few times before I answer. "The orgasms are obvious. They're the reason that I'm here. I want them to stop."

"In order for the orgasms to stop, you need to understand why you are having them."

"I do deal with my stress. Head on. I don't run or hide from it, or pretend it doesn't exist. I dive right in so that I can get it over with and on to the next thing."

Dr. Hamilton nodded before she spoke, "In other words, you rush through one difficult situation so that you can tackle the next difficult situation without rest or stopping to examine what you may have learned or what you can do differently. You do realize that stress can kill you." I never said Dr. H. was Suzy Sunshine.

I didn't say anything, just rubbed my hands across the arms of the chair.

"You have to learn to release your stress and anxiety. That's why you're having orgasms- as a release. Find other ways to "blow" so to speak, and you'll take back your clitoris."

The absurdity of the conversation was so not lost on me.

3

I was eighteen and fresh out of high school when I had my first involuntary orgasm. It was July and David, the man who would become my husband, father of my daughter, and eventually my ex, was away at football camp for his small military college. I was three weeks away from leaving for college myself, and the girls and I were trying to get in as much partying as we legally could.

It was Friday, and I was closing with Mercedes, the older Filipina that I worked with in the accessory section of Bates Department Store. The only people in the mall were high school kids waiting for their movie start times and women in their twenties looking for something to wear to the club later that night. Either way, they weren't in the handbag section of a department store, that was for sure, so Fridays were generally pretty quiet.

The security guard had escorted the last stragglers to the door so that he could lock it behind them, and I was doing the final count on the register when it started. As I counted the till and bagged the cash, I began to feel warm and tingly. My mind was on getting the count right and getting out of there as fast as possible because my best friend Adrienne was going to be outside the employee entrance in her dad's LTD. We called it the Land Ship, and it could comfortably fit seven teenagers (three in the front, and four could squeeze in the back). There would only be three of us that night -Adrienne, Josette, and me.

At first I was caught off guard by the tingling between my legs. I was sure it couldn't be that. I was getting hot and sweaty while counting, and tried to figure out what I had done in the last few minutes that might have triggered the feelings. Nothing. I had been doing nothing but standing around watching the clock and waiting for the store to clear.

I looked around to see that Mercedes was straightening purse racks in the far corner. As the throbbing began to turn into much more, I bent over, crossed my legs, and dropped the cash bag onto the floor. This couldn't possibly be happening. I felt grateful that I had already compartmentalized the bills, checks, and change, and put everything into the green cash bag, ready for drop off at accounting as I dropped the bag on the floor. Mercedes heard the commotion and the till drawer clatter to the floor. She rushed over to see what was wrong. As she reached me, I reached my climax, so I remained bent over with my teeth clenched. God only knows how I managed not to make a sound.

"Are you ok? What's wrong? What happened?" Her accent became thick as the words rushed out of her.

I was embarrassed and shocked, and there was no

way in hell that I was going to tell her what really happened.

"Oh, um. I got a bad cramp," I said when I could finally speak. "Hit me out of the blue. It's gone now, but it was really hurting for a minute."

"Make sure you take some Midol when you get home. I know how bad cramps can get. Had my own, and I've got two girls that have to deal with 'em every month."

I smiled and gathered up all of the evidence of the evening's sales and headed for the accounting window. I couldn't get out of the store fast enough. I didn't want to think about what had just happened. By the time I closed my locker and headed out the door, I'd already placed the incident in the "weird things that happen" category and decided not to worry about it.

4

My life before the involuntary orgasms started again seemed like everyone else's life. Fifteen years of marriage, two years as a divorcee', and sixteen years of parenting were the milestones by which I measured my life. Many of those years were spent climbing the corporate ladder as the perfect working woman cliche'. I loved being Director of Marketing, and was very good at it. I juggled everything with apparent ease. Except, I wasn't so good at the wife/mother thing. My family wanted me to work less and spend more time with them. At the time, I equated working with relaxing. I couldn't see things from their point of view. And it's not because we needed the money. Work, for me, was the grown-up version of a video game. I kept wanting to get to the next career level. And make no mistake, I achieved my own version of success. But my ex had had enough and decided to move forward with a life that didn't include me, which didn't surprise me.

Rachel also saw it coming. Kids are funny like that. It

didn't mean that the divorce was any easier on her, just that she knew her parents were on a very rocky road. What did surprise me was that she chose to live with her father. She picked stability over me, although she tried to reassure me that she knew how much I loved her.

After the final divorce decree, David packed their things and moved to Charlotte, where he started his own tech firm with two part-time employees. The minute he got settled that summer, he found a great private high school for Rachel. The move had David not only rebuilding his career, but also his personal life. That's ex-wife speak for: he started dating again. It appears that newly divorced men don't have the same reservations about getting back out there that newly divorced women have. He was having fun, and I was feeling angry. He was taking my child off to Charlotte, and worse, she wanted to go.

Last fall, I started to feel like Director of Marketing was no longer enough. I worked for a mid-size, but very profitable manufacturing company. We did a lot of regional business and were beginning to take on national clients. I had played a big part in our expansion efforts, but I started feeling like I was on a hamster wheel, and wanted to get off. In fact, one of the reasons I had worked so hard was because David and I had always planned to retire early and open our own individual small businesses (even married, we knew it would be a bad idea to work together). I wanted a neighborhood bookstore and he wanted the small tech company. Looks like we both got what we wished for, we just didn't follow the original plan.

I had begun researching and planning for my bookstore. I told myself that I was just bored and needed entertainment. It was weird coming home to an empty house, even though it had already been that way for over a year. I needed something to keep my mind occupied and the television was wearing thin. I mean, how much reality tv can one person take? Of course, I'm an avid reader, but there was nothing that was really capturing my attention. I knew when I started buying most of my books from the grocery store that I was in trouble.

Book buying used to be a favorite pastime of mine, but it had become quite uninteresting. The big chains were great for variety and coffee, but I missed the days of my youth when I could walk into Brown Books and Mrs. Brown (I know, very original) would recommend a book based on my personality and reading habits, not because someone who bought a book I just read also bought Book X. And that is really how my plans began to fall into place so quickly. I was missing my child, bored at home, and feeling like a hamster at work. With Rachel gone, I often found myself spending time in the room that had the most books in it, my home office, and not because I was doing much work in it.

A few months later my boss was very surprised when I gave him my notice. I was considered a "lifer", except now I was getting paroled. Actually, I was paroling myself and it was scary as hell. I started having the spontaneous orgasms in January, right after I contacted a realtor and began looking for retail space. After many not so great showings, we headed to a spot on Upper King Street. The windows were dirty and dusty and there were broken pieces of wood in the display areas. It was dark and dank and had been empty for years. All I could see was the possibilities. I thought the tingle and wave were signs telling me that this place was for me.

The Perfect Read really is a reflection of the inner me. The store is light and airy with shelves that seem to float around the walls. There are two extra large loveseats in the middle of the store and several large overstuffed chairs sprinkled around the store- all in muted shades of khaki and brown. There are no dark woods, no leather furniture. I wanted a modern feel to the place. At the very back of the store, I have cubicle spaces with Ikea-type desks and chairs. I call it The Writer's Nook. I hope that local writers would feel free to lurk and produce in my store. The checkout desk is in the front, near the door, where I have a great perch from which to read, socialize, ring up sales, or just people watch, in the store or on the street.

The Saturday after my appointment with Dr. Hamilton, I am in the store hanging up "Coming Soon" signs in the display window when this guy in a t-shirt, jeans, steel-toed boots, and a hard hat walks by. He's at least six feet tall, with smooth skin with a reddish-brown hue, and a subtle fade. The sun seems to make his skin glow from the inside out. He glanced at me and gave me a startled wave. I wave back and mutter an appreciative "ugh" as he heads into the coffee shop next door. Within a few minutes he is walking out the store and heading back in the direction from which he came. This time, he just nods. In his hands are two of those coffee dispenser container thingies. Since there is a lot of construction on King Street these days, I assume he is working nearby.

And I'm right, because he comes back a few minutes later to introduce himself. I've gone to the back to bring out some books to start arranging them on shelves near the front when I hear the bell on the door jingle. I poke my head out and I see that it's Mr. Construction Guy.

"Good Morning. Can I help you?" I ask as I head to the front of the store. This time I'm the one with my hands full, but with books instead of coffee.

"Um, sort of. I'm just here to introduce myself. I'm Chris Sullivan and I'm working on a restaurant a few blocks down. I saw you working this morning and thought I'd come in and say 'hello'."

I put the books down on the counter and extend my hand. "I'm Stephanie Price. Nice to meet you."

"Same here Ms. Price. And what are you about to open here? Another shoe store for the ladies?"

I bristle at the question. "Actually, it's a bookstore- you know for folks who *read*. It will just have the look and feel of a boutique." I shouldn't be so snarky since aside from the books in my hands, there are no books on the shelves yet.

If he hears the dismissal in my voice, he doesn't let on. He just smiles and looks around the store as if he is reassessing things. "The decor threw me off. This doesn't look like a traditional bookstore."

"Then it's 'mission accomplished' for me. I wanted a different spin on things. I want folks to relax and hang out and really take their time looking for the 'perfect read'. I want to get to know my customers so that I can make book recommendations, and I want them to get to know and trust me as their book seller. Book buying shouldn't be a nameless/faceless experience."

He breaks out into a huge grin, and that's when I realize that I have been rambling. I skitter behind the counter, as if it can protect me from myself.

"A woman with a passion. I like that."

"And what do you do besides run around getting coffee on Saturday mornings?" I ask, trying to recover from my word fumble.

"I'm working on a restaurant a couple of blocks down. I've worked on a lot of these renovations on Upper King. Did you know that in the past, folks of color owned lots of stores on this end of King?"

"Yep. I'm the latest in a long line of Black Charleston natives, which makes me an expert on Charleston Black history facts. I have to hear that lecture every time she comes downtown."

We both laugh.

"So when is opening day?"

"Three weeks from today."

"Wow- that soon? Well, it looks like you're almost ready. Some books on the shelves and a name on the door would help tip people off. All you've got are those 'Coming Soon' signs in the window. Folks have no idea what's coming. That's why I stopped in. That and to find out about the lady putting up those signs."

I blush, and hope that he can't tell.

"So, Ms. Price, how about you let me call you sometime? I'd like to spend more time talking with you, but I've got to get back to work. I don't want the boss having a hissy fit because I'm gone."

"Um, well. I..." I'm speechless is what I am. I haven't had a date in almost two decades. I don't know how to do this thing.

Before I can finish stumbling over my words, Chris pulls out his business card and slides it across the counter.

"Think about it. If you're interested, that's how you can find me."

With that, he tips his hard hat and heads out the door. I watch him walk away before I pick up his card and read it aloud.

Sullivan Construction.
Christopher Sullivan
Owner and Licensed Contractor

Well now.

I flirt with Chris pretty much every day the following week, and we even start texting in the evenings. It's fun, and safe. We sort of get into a routine: he walks by on his way to get coffee, sticks his head in the door and says hello, and asks me if I needed anything. My response is always the same: "No, but thanks for asking". It's to the point that I'm making sure I'm in the front of the store in the mornings so that I don't miss him.

Strangely enough, even though I'm still stressed as all hell with trying to get the store ready, my waves seem to have lessened. I'm still having them, but they are definitely decreasing in intensity. Dr. Hamilton told me not to get my hopes up about them completely going away. She was all in her psychologist mumbo jumbo about me not dealing with my "real" issues. She thinks my flirtation with Chris was a distraction. She is probably right.

I'm at my usual post, the bookshelves closest to the door when he walks in.

"How you doin' this morning Stephanie?" The grin on his face is just totally adorable.

"I'm good. You look like you just hit the lottery. What's up?"

"Well, whether or not I hit the lottery depends on how you answer my next question."

Uh oh. My heart starts racing. Like we're in some damn 1950's movie and he's going to ask me to the sock hop. I knew it was coming sooner or later. I just thought it would be later.

"What's your question?" I'm cautious, but deliberate.

"No beating around the bush for you- just straight to it, I see," he gives me that smile again . "Well, I just wanted to know if you were free tomorrow night. I'd like to take you to dinner."

And there it is. The ask. My vagina starts contracting and warming up like we've already been engaging in foreplay for the last hour. It's all I can do not to start crossing my legs like I have to pee. Beads of sweat form at my temples, and I just know they'll start rolling down my cheeks before I can get Chris out of my store.

"I...I would love to have dinner with you." I can barely hide my stammer.

"Great. So, text me your address, and I'll pick you up at your house at seven."

"My house? Why can't we just meet at the restaurant? Why do you want to come to my house?" My nerves are getting the best of me and I'm beginning to sound like I've never encountered a man before.

"Because grown men do not *meet* their dates at their destination. They drive to a woman's house, ring her doorbell, present her with flowers, and escort her like a proper gentleman should."

I respond with a simple "oh", hoping that my face is not giving him signs of crazy. The wave is cresting and I don't want to make any sudden moves and have things get out of hand.

"Besides," Sullivan continues, "you're here alone every day. I wouldn't have to go to your home to do you harm. Not that I would. Just stating the obvious."

I sigh deeply, mostly because the wave is almost over, and because I'm embarrassed about my response. I try to make a snappy comeback, except I don't have one.

"Well, I'll text you my address. What restaurant do you have in mind?"

He cocks his head and smiles, which threatens to set me off again. "Not sure yet, but I guarantee it will be good food and great fun. I have to make a good first impression."

I'm ready for him to go so that I can collect myself. "Well, ok then. I'll see you tomorrow evening. And I'll make sure that my 'people' have all of your pertinent information. Just in case."

He laughs his way out of the store.

I can't tell if my sweat is from the orgasm or the fear of a first date.

Hair up? Hair down? Jeans? Pants? A dress? It's becoming too damn much just trying to pull a look together. I decide that a casual dress with platforms will make a statement, but not look like I'm trying too hard.

As I step into the shower, I'm still marveling at the fact that I have given some dude I barely know my address. I mean, sure, in this day of information overload, Chris can probably get some 10 year old kid to Google me and find out everything about me, down to what I had for breakfast, but I still find it unsettling. On the other hand, being picked up for a date feels a bit chivalrous and old school, and I kind of like that.

Once I get my curls dried, get myself lotioned up and dressed, I'm left with 15 minutes to wait. As my anticipation of the doorbell ringing grows, I find myself pacing back and forth from the living room to the kitchen. I consider fixing a drink, but don't want to start things off with a buzz. I'm almost calm when I hear his car pull up in the driveway. And then my clitoris starts to tingle.

Chris wastes no time getting out of the car, taking the steps two at a time. When he presses the doorbell, my uterus starts to contract and I barely have time to grab onto the dining room table. This wave is an intense one. I feel myself sinking just a little, almost into a squat. The pulsing between my legs causes me fear and pleasure at the same time; fear that I would be heard, but leaving me with sweet relief as it ebbs to completion.

A small "oh" escapes from my lips as Chris rings the doorbell for a second time. I need to pull myself together. All the lights are on, and I'm pretty sure he can hear some of my stirrings.

I straighten myself up, pat my hair in place and head for the door. I'm going to have to make a trip upstairs for some dry panties.

I open the door to find Chris leaning against the door jamb like a lanky teenager, with a grin on his face. And then I feel the sweat on my top lip.

"I was wondering if you were trying to figure out how to stand me up."

"Never that." I genuinely smile at him. "Please come in." I clear my throat to get rid of the croaking sounds I seem to be making, and do a casual swipe over my lip.

His casual preppiness is not lost on me. The navy blue polo shirt stretches nicely over his broad shoulders; plain front khakis fit like they were made just for him; and brown driving moccasins top the look off. Nothing to tell the world that he works in construction. Scratch that. That he owns a construction business. But it's his cologne that almost does me in. It's soft and barely noticeable, with hints of musk, citrus, and sandalwood. I swear, I just want to grab him and sniff him until I figure it out.

I put my hand on his back and usher him into the living room. "I hope you didn't have any trouble finding me. I know I live out in the 'country' as my folks like to say."

I don't live in the country, I just live on family property on the outskirts of Mount Pleasant. I like it out here because this isn't a place you're coming unless you have a reason.

"Google maps was great, You live on a real street, so I was good to go." His smile makes me smile.

"Have a seat. I'm ready, but I just need to run upstairs and get my purse. And tell me, what are we in for tonight?"

He rubs his hands together, demonstrating how pleased he is with himself. "We're having a progressive dinner downtown. We'll park, make our way through several courses at different restaurants, and then when we're done, you can decide how we end the night."

A progressive dinner date. That means he's a huge foodie, super thoughtful and wants the night to be special. Or he's working really hard to impress me.

"Sounds like fun. Let me get my bag and then we can get started."

I don't want to race up the stairs like an excited teenager, but I move faster than normal. I need to get my panties off so that we can get the show on the road.

I whirl around my room, taking panties off and putting fresh ones on, remembering to grab my bag off the dresser - my excuse for heading upstairs in the first place. Chris is still standing when I hit the bottom step.

He looks relaxed and amused at the same time. He clears his throat as I head his way.

"Well, I'm ready."

"Um, ahem. Stephanie, um. Your dress."

"What's wrong with my dress?"

"Uh, the back. The back of your dress is sort of jacked up."

I turn as much as my torso will allow, only to see that part of my dress is tucked into the top of my panties. Damn it.

"Excuse me" I say as I back myself through the living room and into the kitchen. I quickly fix my dress and use the toaster to do a face review, finally returning to the living room as gracefully as possible.

"So, let's try this again, minus the mini peep show, shall we."

His laugh is loud and warm. I stop feeling self-conscious immediately.

"Girl, it was the most fun I've had in ages," I giggle as I ran beside Adrienne during our weekly Sunday long run. She is really slowing things down for me this morning because she's more interested in my news than an intense workout.

"So how many restaurants did you guys hit up? Gawd, did he have to roll you out of the car when you got home?"

"Ha! You know I'm southern to my core. Ate like a bird."

"You know that birds eat like 10 times their weight daily, or some shit like that."

We both laugh. It's a stupid old joke between us that we had kept alive since high school.

"Seriously though, tell me how it went down."

"Well, after I pulled my dress out of my panties, we headed downtown and started with drinks at Virginia's on King. We had our appetizer at Coast Bar and Grill, ate surf and turf at Hall's Chophouse, and then finished up at Cupcake DownSouth for dessert. After all that, we decided to walk off some of that ridiculous goodness."

"Enough about the food, I need to hear about *him*. Where's he from, how's his business doing? Is he funny or a meathead?" Because Adrienne has a serious "need to know". It's what makes her a great newswoman.

"Girl, he's a local. Left home to attend college at Howard and became an architect. Started a firm in DC, got married and divorced a couple of times, no kids, though he has a stepson that he's still pretty close to. Came back home after the second divorce, selling off his company, and because his dad was needing a little help as he got older.

"So, he's got strong family connections. That's good."

"Yep. His dad's home needed major repairs and he had time on his hands. Says he went a bit overboard on the upgrades. When he finished with his dad's house, one of his dad's neighbors asked him to work on her house, so that is pretty much how his company began."

"A man good with his hands. That's important. But how did he manage to get out of two marriages with *no* kids?"

"First marriage was right out of college. Lasted about 3 years. Second marriage was in his early thirties and they were together for 10 years. He loves his stepson as if he were his own, and is happy to have a great relationship with him."

"How very zen of him."

"Come on girl, don't do that. So far, he really seems like a stand up guy."

"Defending him already are we? Hmm, wonder what makes him so special that I can't make fun of him yet?"

We laugh and as we round the corner toward our parked cars.

"On a serious note, how did you do with your orgasm situation last night? Did you have a difficult night?"

Adrienne is the only person I've told about my orgasms besides my doctors.

"Yeah, I had an episode just as he was ringing the doorbell, but I actually didn't have any problems during the night. The rest of the night was good."

"Huh. What do you think made the difference. I know how nervous you were about the whole date thing."

I'm ready with the answer because I've been thinking about it since he dropped me off last night. "He's easy to be around and he makes me laugh. He doesn't know me, so I don't have to worry about being anything but myself. He only knows what I've told him so far. It feels kind of freeing."

"Well, that is saying something. I haven't seen you this relaxed in ages. As a matter of fact, this is the first time you don't look like you're about to blow a gasket, and not an orgasmic one, since you and The Arrogant Ass split."

Adrienne has refused to call David by his name since the day I told her we were splitting up. She's never forgiven him for not fighting for us, no matter how hard I try to convince her that there was nothing to fight for. And that whole girlfriend a few months after moving didn't help matters. She's super romantic and has been happily married for the last 20 years to the first guy she dated out of college. In fact, Jeff's face still lights up when she walks into a room, as if they just fell in love. If she were someone else, I'd be totally jealous.

"Come on Adrienne, aren't you exaggerating just a bit. You sound like I've been tense for years."

"Girl please. You like to think your overachieving personality contributed to the situation, but you know what I believe- David was just looking for an excuse to exit because he couldn't match you professionally."

As my best friend, Adrienne is overly and irrationally protective.

"Here we go again. Look Adrienne, I'm hungry, so I'm heading to Starbucks for coffee and a muffin. What are you and Jeff doing tonight?."

"The boys both have dates tonight, so Jeff and I are gonna finish off some weed we found in Alex's room last month. His dad grounded him for a couple of weeks, but since they'll both be out of the house for the night, we decided to take a toke, for old time's sake."

"Really?! Y'all smoking weed like teenagers? You two are gonna be trouble when those boys go to college in a couple of years."

"Girl, I hope so! And no, we're not smoking the weed. I'll probably bake a small batch of cookies or brownies. I'll hide them so the boys won't get to them. Which will serve them right. And speaking of food, you shouldn't be hungry after all that damn food you ate last night Greedy Gert."

I laugh and shake my head at Adrienne as I pull my key out of the pocket of my capris and let myself in the Jeep. "Really? Greedy Gert? That's the best you got?"

"Go 'head home. You know I'm right. And you need to

stop consuming all that processed sugar. That's probably part of your problem."

"This coming from the woman who's about to make weed cookies," I said with a laugh as I crank up the Jeep and throw it in reverse.

By the time I get home and got shower, I'm ready for some down time. The store opening is a couple of weeks away, and I still have a few marketing things to follow through on. Adrienne works as an executive producer at one of the local stations and managed to get a crew assigned to cover the grand opening. Economic recovery meets old school bookstore meets the new millennium kind of story. I'm grateful for the exposure, but I know that I need to have a multi-pronged approach in order to be successful. My plan is to spend the afternoon setting up social media accounts for the store when my cell phone rings. It's Chris.

I'm surprised at the call so early after our date, but I'm also a little bit pleased. As I press the button to accept the call, I wonder if maybe he is the desperate type and I just didn't pick up on it yet.

"Hello?"

"Hey, Stephanie. How are things?"

"Um, good Chris? How are you? What's up? Did I leave something in your car?"

His laugh is throaty and genuine.

"You think I'm stalking you, huh?"

"Uh, no, well, kinda. I don't know," I laugh as well. No need to lie.

"Well, I know we just saw each other last night, but I wanted to call and let you know that I had a great time. Also, tickets just dropped in my lap for the Will Downing concert tonight. I just wondered if you wanted to go."

"Really? You got tickets to see Will? Tonight? And you took me to dinner last night in case the date was a dud you wouldn't have to waste your night listening to Will with someone you potentially had nothing in common with, huh?" This is my attempt at being casual, flirty, and funny, but I'm starting to sound just awkward.

"Yeah, uh. No," he laughs. "My boy got tickets for him and his wife, and since she went into labor last night, I'm pretty sure they won't be needing them tonight. You know, with having just had their first baby and all."

I can hear the sneer in his voice.

"Oh. Well congrats to *your boy*. What makes you think I like Will Downing?"

"You didn't ask me to change the station from the Watercolors channel on Sirius last night. I figured you were cool with it."

"Will is more heart and soul R&B than he is jazz."

"So, you do like Will Downing's music?" He's making it clear to me that he isn't scared of a little banter. I like it.

"Actually, I love Will Downing's music. I own every album he's ever made. Even the Christmas one."

"And yet, you don't already have tickets for tonight's

show." He's right. I've been so focused on the store that when I remembered about the concert tickets were sold out.

"Which brings me back to my original question. Would you like to go with me to the concert tonight? Unless you have some rule about having a second date right after the first date."

"I have no dating rules as of yet. Maybe you can help me create a list."

I find myself in the sunroom, stretching out on the sofa. I throw my legs over the arm of the sofa and look up at the ceiling as we continue our conversation.

"Well, would you like to work on the list at dinner before the concert, or should we just do drinks afterwards?"

"Dinner again? Dude I had to run 6 miles with my girlfriend this morning to try to undo some of the damage we did last night. That was a lot of food."

"It was, but we paced ourselves." We both laugh at that.

"So, what are you up to this morning besides making plans for tonight? I thought small business owners work 24/7. Everyone keeps telling me that I'm not going to have a life for the first three to five years."

"It's kind of true, and it's not. But it is Sunday. Even God rested. It's all about setting parameters. You can't enjoy your work or your personal life if they're always bleeding into each other."

The conversation is getting good, so I get up from the sofa to go grab a bottle of water out of the fridge.

"Well, as a new proprietor, I know that I'll be at the store a lot. I have a small part-time staff ready to roll on opening day, but really it's pretty much going to be me. I'm scared out of my mind because I really want this place to be a success. I mean, financial success would be great, but I'm more interested in establishing a community meeting place, especially for the aspiring writers."

"Oh, so you have a thing for writers?"

"I wouldn't say I have a 'thing' for writers. I just have an appreciation for creatives. And writers are, of course, a big part of that population. As a kid, my mom would send us outside to play and I'd grab a book or two, and hit the patio furniture under the shade. Reading was play for me."

"I get that. I read the entire Hardy Boys series one summer."

"Get out of here! I had the entire Hardy Boys and Nancy Drew series. Got them for Christmas and saved them for the summer. Finished both series about halfway through summer vacation, so I started them again. I can't remember doing anything that summer other than reading. I carry a book with me everywhere I go, because of all the reading I did that summer." I'm rambling again.

"So what do you read now?"

"Everything. Mostly. I read a lot of chick lit when my daughter was young. It was easy to get through. Romance in my teens through my 20s. Then a lot of murder mysteries after my divorce."

"You don't say."

"Hey, it was just the 'season' I was in. So, what's the last book you read?"

"The history of architecture in Charleston. As a matter of fact, I'm still reading it. But for fun, I'm into biographies. Just finished Donald Driver's book. Cool dude. A man of integrity."

We talk for a solid hour, and before I know it, I'm rushing him off the phone so that I can get a few things done before the concert.

At the end of the night. I realize that I haven't had an orgasm all day.

10

I'm in the shop a few days later getting the furniture delivered and set up when the familiar warmth begins to radiate from my groin. The throbbing starts after I get into it with the delivery guy who says it's not his responsibility to assemble the table legs. I march into the office to find my copy of the purchase order, while dialing the number for the store where I bought the furniture from so I could speak to the manager, when I realize what's happening. Once I reach my office, I immediately slow down and take a deep breath.

I'm so focused on my breathing and trying to slow things down in my head that I almost don't notice that the symptoms have subsided. I think that maybe the stuff Doc Hamilton is trying to teach me is finally working. Until I find myself on hold for 15 minutes. I can barely keep myself together when the manager finally takes my call. I'm about to go hard in the paint with ripping the manager a new asshole when the pulsing began between my legs.

I start to dance, as if I have to use the bathroom. That's the wrong move. Moving around begins to make things worse.

"Look," I say through clenched teeth, "my contract says that your men will put the legs on the tables. Do you need me to fax you a copy over?"

"I'm sorry Ms. Price, just let me find..."

"Ugh, uh, ohhh."

"Ma'am? I didn't quite make out what you said."

"Ummmmm, ahhhh... yeah."

"Excuse me?"

"Have. You. Have you found it yet?" I force the question out of me as I grip the edge of my desk with my free hand.

"Uh, yeah, just a sec. Ah, yes. Right here. It says assemble legs for four tables. So, I'll give my driver a call and have them get right on that. I'm really sorry for the inconvenie...."

"Bye. Thanks"

I hang up as the last of the wave crests over me. I fall back into my chair, contemplating whether pressing my hands between my legs will staunch the tide washing over me or make it worse. When I look up, I see Chris coming towards me.

"Steph? What's wrong? I came by to see if everything was ok because I saw a crew of men hanging out in front but didn't see you. What happened? Are you in pain?"

Talking is not an option for me at this point because I am embarrassed beyond belief. I don't know what to say, so I simply continue to slump and wave my hand to shoo him away.

" What's going on? How can I help?"

"I'm fine." It comes out as a growl, and I see a look of confusion pass over his face. I collect myself and start again.

"I'm sorry Chris. I'm fine. I just had a moment. A stomach thing. Don't worry. Everything is ok." I know I don't sound very convincing, but there is no way I'm going to tell him about my 'problem' right now. I have too much on my plate, and figuring out how to explain my spontaneous orgasms is not high on the To Do list.

"I've got to get these guys squared away so that I can finish setting up. Grand opening is on Friday and I feel like I'm not going to be ready in time. I'm really fine, it's just a stomach thing. Can I call you this evening when I get home and settled?" I can't get him out of there fast enough. The look on his face tells me that he isn't believing the whole stomach story.

"Um, yeah, Steph. You can call me this evening, I guess. Just thought you needed some help."

Chris does a slow exit from the office. He seems a little hurt, but I can't worry about that right now.

I grab a bottle of water from my mini-fridge and drink half of it before I feel that I'm ready to face anyone else. By the time I walk into the main part of the store, the guys from the furniture place were laughing as they pulled table tops and legs out of boxes. Finally, I think, as I perch on the counter at the front of the store. My thoughts are all over the place, as I contemplate whether it's time to tell Chris about my condition.

I dial Adrienne shortly after the evening news goes off. I'm in a foul mood, but it's a good time to catch her. She'll be wrapping things up at the station, which means her work day will be pretty much over (unless there was some breaking news shit) and I can catch her before she gets home and into Mommy Mode.

"What up heifer?" Caller ID means that Adrienne never has to be polite when answering the phone unless she doesn't recognize the number.

"Hey girl. What you doing?"

"Same thing I'm always doing after the broadcast, grabbing my crap to get the hell up outta here. How's life Boss Lady?"

"Ugh, girl, you won't believe what happened to me today." I can always get right down to it with Adrienne. "Chris came in and saw me at the tail-end of an episode."

"Oh shit. Was it a light one or a super intense one?"

"It was the super intense kind. Didn't seem to want to

let up." Truth is, I had two more orgasms before the guys left the store, and one more on my way home.

"Hmm. Well, I'm no Dr. Hamilton, but I can honestly say that you seem to have the intense kind when you are on Stress Level 10. And they seem worse when it's a situation you can't control. What did you say to Chris when he saw you?"

"Thanks for the diagnosis," I say with sarcasm. "Chris didn't say much. I tried to get him out of there as quickly as possible. I wasn't ready to explain things to him and then have him think I'm some kind of freak, or worse, that I'm a real sex fiend or something."

"Speaking of sex, you guys have been seeing each other practically every day for the last two weeks. How have you managed not to get aroused? Can you still get aroused?"

"Yes, Girl, I can still get aroused. Damn! And who says I haven't gotten aroused around him? That man's kisses are sweet. We've kept them pretty PG though. I told him I want to take things slow, so he's been a gentleman the entire time."

"Look Mama, you're too old to be worrying about your reputation. If you want to have sex with the man, do that. But you need to tell him what's up before you do. What happens if you start to cum and he hasn't even gotten your clothes off? That shit would be hard to explain. Funny as hell, but hard to explain."

Adrienne's laugh is so loud and long, I pull the phone away from my ear.

"Shut up heifer. I'm gonna tell him. I'm just going to wait until after the opening on Friday. He'll be joining us for drinks afterwards, by the way."

"Good. I can't wait to meet him. I need to see this dude for myself. And speaking of Friday, the camera crew will be there by 5:00, they'll roll some B footage, we'll do a quick interview, more footage of us celebrating, and then they'll be out."

"Thanks for this Adrienne. The store can use all the publicity it can get. I'm really nervous about the opening. Does anyone buy physical books anymore? Someone has to right? People still keep writing them."

"Yes people buy books, or you wouldn't be opening a bookstore. Your bookstore is more about the experience, not the actual selling of books. Don't forget that. You're catering to the hipsters of Charleston. Vinyl records have made a comeback, and bookstores that aren't big box stores will too.

"Look, I've gotta go. I'm home and I've got to let those boys and their daddy have my undivided attention for like five minutes or they start to pout. I'll call you tomorrow."

"OK, cool. And tell the boys Auntie says hey. Haven't seen them in a while, so maybe we should do a big dinner soon."

"Sounds good. I'll holla later."

"K. Bye."

As I end the call, I plod into the kitchen to grab some guacamole and some chips to munch on while I finish working on the plans for opening night. It's the home stretch, and I'm ready to finally make this thing happen.

I 'm at the store finishing the setup of my office when the front door dings. When I get to the front of the store, my mother is leaning on the counter running her hands over the wood. She looks impressed.

"Mama," I exclaim, as I moved towards her to give her a hug. I haven't seen her since she got back from her cruise last weekend, which is why we scheduled lunch in the first place.

Her hug is tight and warm. No one hugs like my mother.

"Hey baby. I didn't want to wait 'til Friday to see this place. And since we're having lunch down here, I came early to check things out for myself."

"Well, as you can see, we're pretty much done. Carly, my assistant, started on Monday, and I have a couple of part timers that will be working as well. They've been in to help set up, but they're all college students, so I'm trying to give them a few extra hours."

Carly is adding some books on the shelves, but comes

over when I call her name. I introduce my mom to Carly and then give her the grand tour. By the time we reach my office, I can tell that my mother is thoroughly impressed.

"It really looks good in here baby. A little modern feeling, but I like it. I thought you would have some of those brown leather library couches in here like in your house, but I love this."

My mother never misses an opportunity to mention the leather sofas in my home. She feels like they bring the mood down and make the room dark. But, after years of having white furniture, even when Rachel was a toddler (who does that?) I couldn't care less.

"Yeah, so how was your trip Mom? Did you have fun?" I ask, changing the subject.

"Girl, I had a blast. Two weeks on a ship traveling through the Panama Canal? Getting served breakfast, lunch, and dinner? Stopping and sightseeing? What more could a retired woman ask for? You really should come with us when we do the Mediterranean next year."

"Um, really Mama? I'm pretty sure I won't be able to take two weeks off at one time next year."

"What's the point of being your own boss if you can't set your own schedule? That doesn't make any sense."

I shake my head, "Let's head to lunch Mama and I can explain to you why leaving for vacation for two weeks when you've just started a business is not a good idea."

By the time we're seated and place our orders at Virginia's on King, Mom has given me the King Street History lesson for the millionth time, picked a couple of stores to go into on our way back, and ranted about why her favorite downtown store is no longer in business. I'm hungry and ready to chew my arm off. Mom doesn't notice.

"So how is my granddaughter doing?" she asks as the server settles our plates on the table, "I haven't seen her in weeks. And she doesn't call me. Why do teenagers seem to be so incredibly busy these days? These newfangled parents start over scheduling kids in the womb."

"Rachel is busy Mom. She got the lead in the spring musical, and she's completing applications for that theater workshop she wants to attend this summer. Plus, she just got her car, so, you know, she's learning to balance responsibility and freedom. Not easy."

"That doesn't mean she can't call her grandmother. When she was here, I saw her every week and talked to her several times a week. Charlotte is just three hours away and the phones still work as far as I know."

"They do, but you know, she's figuring things out. She's finishing up her junior year so she is realizing she only has so much time left to be a kid. David is doing a good job with her, and I really think that is what you're getting at."

"I don't know why you let her go with him for high school anyway. What happened to mothers having custody in a divorce? All of this back and forth has to be confusing for a kid. Moms got them during the school year and dads who weren't trifling got the summers. Now you got kids splitting weeks between houses. It's too much."

"Mom, we have been over this. It's best for Rachel to have access to both her parents. She learns different things from each of us. And regardless of what you think about him, David is not a bad parent. I'm not going to let you do that."

Mom is ruffled, but doesn't back down. "He's a good parent, but he didn't fight for you and the marriage. I'm never going to forgive him for that."

"Mom, I could have fought for the marriage just as much as he could have. We're good. Everybody is not meant to be married. I may be one of those people. And I'm ok with it."

"Which I do not understand because your dad and I had a good marriage. I thought we set a good example for you."

"You did. And marriage was great for you guys. Look, let's not do this. I'm stressed enough with the opening on Friday. Are you and the Lunch Ladies coming?"

The Lunch Ladies are my mom's best friends. There are four of them, and they have been together since I was in middle school. Rachel gave them the name Lunch Ladies because when she would have a school holiday, she'd spend it with my mom and have lunch with "the ladies". The name stuck.

"I'm not sure how many will make it, but you know I am going to be there and looking fierce."

"Ugh, this is not Ebony Fashion Fair. Please Mom, no hats and no ritzy get ups. You're too much."

"I can't help it if you kids don't know anything about style these days. Honey, I've never left the house half-stepping and I am not about to start now."

We both laugh because indeed that is true. Mom prides herself on her sense of style and flair. She still turns heads with her short, curly fro, high heels, and dewy skin. She claims that the secret to great looking skin was drinking water, and plenty of it.

We enjoy the rest of our lunch while I listen to tales of her latest trip. On the walk back to The Perfect Read, I catch myself thinking that Mom and Chris would really like each other and can't help but smile.

13

_____

The next few days are consumed by opening night preparations. Chris is only able to stop in once because his renovation is at a critical point.

I consider telling Chris about riding the wave, but don't because I haven't had another episode all week. I think that maybe I'm starting to get past this thing. I mean, I've been calm, even with the stress of the opening. David and Rachel are coming with the new girlfriend and I'm not even freaking out about it. Chris meeting my entire crew on the same night, while it gives me pause, does not freak me out.

I decide to be brave and invite Chris over for dinner the eve of the opening. We've been having such great conversations, it just feels right and comfortable. I don't think about the possibility of what could come next for us.

I make a lasagne with lots of cheese and Italian sausage, open a bag caesar salad combo, make a pound cake for dessert, and pick up some vanilla bean ice cream. I'm a runner for a reason.

I want the evening to feel casual and fun, so I put my hair up, throw on my favorite message tee, and my super comfy jeans with all the stretch. Chris has seen me in a getup similar to this many times in the past few weeks, so I don't feel self conscious at all.

The doorbell rings at precisely seven o'clock, just as I finish setting the table on the patio and taking the pitcher of iced tea out of the fridge.

Chris greets me with a warm one handed hug and a potted plant.

"Well, hello", I say as I step aside to let him in.

"Hey lady", Chris replies, giving me the once over, "you look relaxed."

"Don't let the look fool you, I've been in the kitchen for the last two hours. And that is not something that I do. Actually, I've made you the one dish that I can actually cook, so I hope you enjoy it."

"Wait, so you don't cook? Yet you invited me to dinner and gave it a go anyway? How very modern of you, for a southern woman."

"No, I don't cook regularly," I say with a smirk, "but, I can bake my ass off. And that counts here in the south."

Chris chuckles as he continues to stand in the foyer.

The way he is looking at me makes me a little nervous and I feel full of jitters. "Where are my manners? Come in, have a seat on the patio. Dinner is ready."

"Actually, since you have gone to all the trouble of making me your one dish, I need to at least help you bring the food out. Where can I put this plant?"

"Let me take that", I replied. "You can follow me into the kitchen since you'd like to help."

I grab the plant and head into the kitchen, while Chris trails behind me. We make quick work of getting the food out to the patio. By the time we're seated, the sun starts to set over the marsh.

The conversation over dinner is fun and engaging. That, in combination with the food and wine has me feeling relaxed. So when Sade's voice comes over the speakers, I don't hesitate to grab Chris's hand and invite him to dance.

We don't talk as we sway to "King of Sorrow", and as he holds me close, his smell begins to make me slightly lightheaded. Or maybe it's the wine. Either way, when I stand on my tiptoes to kiss him, I'm met with a warm, soft response.

How luscious and soft his lips feel! As I move my hands up to his head to bring him in even closer, his arms encircle my waist and gently press me against him. I can feel myself getting warm as each moment passes. All of my senses are being pleasantly assaulted as we kiss and dance.

Chris breaks the kiss as the song ends, but he continues to hold me and I press my face to his chest. We stand there for a few moments. Just breathing and hugging.

It's too quiet, too intimate, too comfortable, so I step back and move towards the table. My body is slowly coming down from his touch, and I need to catch my breath. We have never exchanged more than a casual kiss and church hugs. But I'm wanting more than a church hug right now.

I want to feel his skin next to mine. I want to run my hands along that broad chest and back. As my thoughts began to expand, I felt the familiar rise of warmth. Chris has begun silently helping me with the dishes, while glancing at me with a sly expression. In that moment, I'm scared about what comes next.

I start breathing in for a count of four, and out for a count of four. I need to try to get things under control.

"Is everything ok?"

I look over at Chris and notice that he looks concerned.

"Um, yeah, why do you ask?" I head to the kitchen as I speak.

Chris follows me with a wary look. "Well, you started breathing funny, and got kind of still."

I open the dishwasher and begin to pile in the dishes. I need to keep moving because I'm not sure what will happen if I get close to him again.

When Chris comes up behind me and wraps his arms around me, I let out an audible moan. The minute he touches me, it feels like my body catches fire. I know that the wave will be rolling in, and that I won't be able to stop it. I want the wave. But I want it with foreplay and penetration. And as quickly as I have that thought, I have the first explosion. It's small, but powerful. Chris's groin pressing against my butt doesn't help matters either. I try to move, but am afraid. So I stand stiffly and hope that I can keep my body from reacting.

Another small explosion goes off in my clitoris. It feels good, but wrong. I sidestep Chris and bolt out of the kitchen. I pop again a few seconds later as I hit the top of the stairs. By the time I get to my room and close the door, I barely have time to make it to my bed. I grab a pillow and place it between my legs while sweet ecstasy pulses throughout my body. Those 20 seconds leave me sweaty, with a racing heartbeat. I'm relieved and ashamed at the same time. How could my body do this to me? I lay on the bed for several minutes while my heart rate slows and my breathing returns to normal. My thoughts are all over the place. I want an orgasm like that with Chris and yet, I have nothing left in me. I'm spent.

Chris! Shit, I left him downstairs.

When I return to the kitchen, everything is neat and tidy and put away. I find a note on the table that says "Call me and let me know if you are ok."

14

I wait until the following morning to send Chris a text message asking him to please show up for the opening and that I will explain everything to him after the event. I've been up half the night trying to figure out what to say, and decide against saying anything over the phone. He doesn't respond, but I can't blame him. I'll worry about it later. Right now, I need to get out of the door and make sure everything at the bookstore is on point. I pack my clothes, shoes, makeup bag, two hand towels, a washcloth and soap because I'll be getting dressed in the employee restroom at the store.

The day is spent putting last minute touches on everything. Polishing tables, cleaning reflective surfaces, moving furniture around, and dropping the temperature on the air conditioner so that it's near freezing because once bodies started piling it, things will warm up quickly. The caterer assures me that the hors d'oeuvres will be in place thirty minutes ahead of time, and that the bartender will begin serving promptly at 6:00. While I'm expecting at least fifty people, I have enough food for twice that.

As the day wears on, I find myself hovering near the store window. I'm hoping to catch Chris walking by to pick up lunch or coffee or both. But I never see him. The disappointment rolls into my nervous opening day energy, and I repeatedly tell myself that he will show up and I'll have an opportunity to explain everything to him. Except, his radio silence is making me very unsure.

By the time 4:30 rolls around, Mom starts calling me every 10 minutes and asking if I'm dressed yet. The fact that I'm getting dressed at the store is not sitting well with her. By 5:00, I assure her that I will be ready and that she needs to stop calling me. I put my phone on silent and head to my office to do a last minute review of my checklist.

Once seated at my desk, I lean back in my chair and let my eyes close for just a minute. I realize that I have not stopped moving since I got to the store. The silence feels wonderful and I feel myself about to drift when I hear a tap on the door jamb. I open my eyes to see Chris, looking sexy in a pair of jeans, loafers and white button down with the sleeves rolled halfway up.

"Hey," I say, as the smile reaches my eyes.

"Hey," he replies with a hint of hesitancy.

"You came." I look down at my desk, as my embarrassment rises to the surface.

"I did. I said I would support you tonight, so I'm here. But I'm also really interested in hearing your explanation about what happened last night. I'm trying to figure out if you are playing games with me or is there something else going on."

"Playing games with you?" My embarrassment is becoming something else. "Why would I play games with you?"

"You tell me. Why does a grown woman run upstairs after a great dinner and a romantic moment? Why does she send me a vague text the following morning? I wasn't trying to press you for anything further, and at any point you could have asked me to back off and go home. Which I would have done. So yeah, you tell me why you would be playing games."

I take a deep breath to slow my internal processes down. I owe this man an apology. Whether I like it or not.

Before I can open my mouth, Adrienne comes barreling in my office, looking official and curious at the same time.

She walks over to Chris with her hand outstretched. "So, you must be Chris". Her grin is ridiculous.

"I am. You must be the best friend." His smile is genuine.

Meanwhile, I'm silent and rooted to the floor.

"I am. I'm Adrienne. And as happy as I am to meet you Chris, I've got to get Steph ready for her closeup." She then truly looks at me and gasps. "Girl, why are you not dressed?"

"I, well, I was..." I trail off. I'm tired and embarrassed and now about to be late for my own event. It feels like too much.

And then David walks in with Rachel and some deep dark chocolate Amazon warrior. Calling this chick gorgeous is an insult. Rachel gives a quick hug to Adrienne and then bounds toward me and squeezes me hard. I haven't been to Charlotte in several weeks because I've been busy, so there is no one I'm more happy to see at that moment.

I can't stop staring at the beautiful woman while hugging my child, though. Damn. Of course David would walk in my place with some damn supermodel and a stupid grin on his face. This is my night! Why can't he just let me have this?

Instead of saying hello, David opens with "Who is this guy?" and shoots his thumb at Chris. Adrienne gives me a "what an ass" look.

"This 'guy' is my friend, Chris Sullivan. Chris, this is my ex, David."

They do a Black man fist bump exchange, just as my mom comes barreling in the office.

"Well, well, well. It's crowded in here. Why didn't you tell me that you were having a pre-game function?"

"Hey Mama," is all I can get out because everyone starts to address her or move to hug her. When she gets to Chris, she throws her arms around him and asks "who is this good looking young man, and is he here for me?"

Carly then joins the crowd with a fretful look on her face.

"Um, excuse me Stephanie, but Andrew just called, and he's not coming in. He broke his elbow skateboarding on his way to class this morning. He's pretty drugged up and will probably be out for a few days."

I let Rachel out of my grip, but kept one arm around her. "No problem Carly. I'm sure you and I can handle things. Since it's an open house, we probably won't have a ton of sales tonight anyway." Look at me handling things, I think to myself..

"Um, well, also, the sink in the men's room won't stop running. One of the caterers thinks he may have stripped the handle when he was turning the water off after washing his hands. I called a plumber, but it will be an hour before he gets here."

My heart starts beating faster. What made me think I can do this? That I can be a business owner? And why the hell am I having a grand opening for a damn bookstore?

"How many plumbers did you call after that Carly?" my tone is clipped.

"Oh. I. Well, I didn't..." Her voice trails off.

"Well, I'm going to need you to-" my impending rant is interrupted by Chris's voice. It's clear that I'm about to go off the rails.

"I can can probably help you with the sink. Let me get my tools out of the truck." He's walking out of the door by the time I managed to get "thanks" out of my mouth. Carly follows him out, while the others look uncomfortable.

"Stephanie, you really need to get dressed. My crew is here and ready to get set up. Your live segment will start right before the weather. We don't have much time to get lighting and angles right. I need you to hop to it!"

"Wait, did you just say live Adrienne?" My voice begins to sound high and squeaky. "I thought we were taping."

"Oh, yes, girl. We were, but then my producer thought a live shot would be great. A great neighborhood resurgence story. Look, the economy's picking up. All that. Plus, it's a slow news day."

"You could have told me earlier!" I yell.

Adrienne doesn't miss a beat, "Yeah, everyone get out, let Stephanie get dressed. Rachel, how about you show your dad and, um"

"Lexi. Her name is Lexi," David volunteers, as he saunters towards me to give me a hug. "We wanted to get here early and make proper introductions, but it looks like you still have a lot to handle."

I reach out to shake Lexi's hand. "It's a pleasure to meet you. I'm running behind, but we can definitely talk later."

"Sure, I'd love that." She's gracious and elegant even as I give her the bum's rush.

"Rachel, please show your dad and Lexi around. I'll catch up with you guys in a few." I can feel the wave flowing in and I need to get them out quickly.

Adrienne's spidey senses start tingling because she gets everyone out of the office, closes the door, and then turns and grabs me by the shoulders.

"You good girl?"she asks.

"Nah. I'm..."

"Yeah, I can see, looks like things are heating up for you." She reaches into her big purse and pulls out a bottle of water and a brownie. "Have you had anything to eat?"

"Not since lunch. Too excited". I'm breathing deeply and talking slowly.

"Well, here. Eat this and drink some water. You just need to get something in your system. It'll help calm you down. I'm gonna head out and give the crew some instructions. See you in a few."

She gives me a quick hug and doesn't wait for a response.

I don't realize how hungry I am until I take the first bite of the brownie. I finish it off in a few bites, drink some of the water and head to the bathroom to change. I realize that the food has helped because I'm feeling much calmer.

When I finally finish dressing, I have less than ten minutes before the live broadcast begins. I put on my lipstick, and do a final adjustment on my dress. One deep inhale, and I open the door into the store. The sound of jazz coming from the speakers surrounds me and mingles with the steady hum of voices in the room. The place has filled up quickly. Part of me is really surprised at the turnout. But this is Charleston. Free food and drink are a sure-fire way to draw people in.

I notice that Adrienne's camera guy has set up in the creative nook. I think it's the perfect backdrop for an interview. I head over to the set-up when Chris appears at my side. He puts his hand on my elbow and guides me to an unoccupied corner. I know what he wants, but this isn't the time.

"Chris, don't say anything. I know we need to talk. I just can't get into it right now." I decide to beat him to the punch.

"I know that Stephanie, but we do need to talk about it. The bathroom sink is fixed and you're good to go. I just want a promise from you that we'll talk tonight when everything is all wrapped up."

"That's fair Chris. It'll happen. Right now, I've got to get this show on the road." I touch him on the shoulder as I head back to the interview spot. Adrienne is waving me over and is starting to get impatient.

By the time I reach her, she looks like she wants to wring my neck. "Damn girl, what is going on with you and Chris? He looks like he's trying to figure out if he needs to stay or run. What did you do?"

"I didn't *do* anything Adrienne," I hiss as her camera guy begins looking for a spot to place the microphone on me. He decides my shoulder is a good place and asks me to a run it from the outside of my sleeveless dress to the inside of my lapel.

"Oh no, you didn't, well, blow your stack on him, did you?" Adrienne stage whispers.

"Blow my stack? Really?"

"Well, did you?"

"Look, not now." I'm starting to get hot from the lights and Adrienne is cranking me up instead of keeping me calm.

When the camera guy reaches over and gives me a tissue, I realize that I'm starting to sweat. A lot.

"Adrienne, how much longer? These lights are cooking me."

Adrienne's eyes get a little wide as her face registers what is happening.

I'm starting to feel light headed. My first thought is that the brownie has only teased my stomach and that hunger is going to do me in. And then I can feel it. My vagina starts to heat up from the outside in. I am wearing granny panties and no pantyhose because I didn't want chance things with friction happening between my legs all night. I have prepared for the worst case scenario. But I'm wrong.

Adrienne puts her hand over her mic and whispers in my ear: "I thought the brownie would calm you down. It's got marijuana in it."

"What hell Adrienne!" A few heads turn in our direction.

"Mic's going hot Adrienne, you guys ready?" The camera guy was giving us a warning.

I give Adrienne a killer look. I have every intention of pinching the shit out of Adrienne as soon as we're done. I feel a drop of sweat roll down the small of my back. The heat between my legs is getting even more intense. I stand with one leg crossed tightly over the other. I just need to get through the next couple of minutes and I'll be fine.

Sweat beads form on the side of my face and my upper lip. I gently dab them away with the tissue that I had the foresight to grab on my way out of my office. I don't want to make any grand moves in case I set things off.

Adrienne begins with her intro, but the sound becomes muted due to the pounding in my ears. It's like my entire body is a furnace and radiating heat. I hear something about an appreciation for analog in a digital world, discovering great reads, and books in your hands, but by the time Adrienne asks her first question, I'm feeling like I'm going to erupt. This is not a wave, but hot, molten lava oozing out of me.

Somehow I get through the first couple of questions, but the meltdown reaches critical mass when my sweating increases. When the throbbing in my clitoris intensifies, I shift my stance. That just makes things worse.

"So, Stephanie, tell us what will make your bookstore different from the big box stores?"

"Well, we..." Oh no. This really can't happen.

"Uh, we focus on the reader's experi..." At this point, I start looking around for something to grab ahold of. I start to panic, and it's clear that something is out of the ordinary.

"You were saying about the reader's experience." Adrienne never breaks out of reporter mode.

"Oh God! I. Oh. Ohhhh." My bottom lip starts to tremble. I yank the mic through my sleeve, pull the mic pack from my belt and drop the entire thing on the floor. I push people aside as I unsteadily cut through the crowd to my office. Low moans are coming from deep within, but I sound far away to myself.

I grab hold of the doorjamb and bend over and that is when the first wave crests. My moan is unbelievably loud. The stuff pornos are made of. Within seconds, strong arms grab me and pull me into the office. The arms hold onto me as I make it to the desk and surrender to what was coming next.

"Oh. My. Go-. This can't be. Uhhh" My pelvis jerks on its own. There is nothing I could do but let it finish. The arms never let me go. By now, the sweat is mixing with my tears as my moans turn into whimpers, which eventually become crying.

I slumped down to the floor when I realize that Chris's arms have been the ones to hold me during the most embarrassing moment of my life. He sits down beside me and pulls my head to his chest while my body continues to shake from the intense crying and aftershocks.

Adrienne and my mom are the first ones in the room with David and Rachel right behind them. At least Lexi has the good sense not to come in. I begin to cry harder when I see them.

Adrienne sits on the floor on the other side of me and grabs my hand.

"Sweetie, I'm so sorry. I thought that the weed would help. I didn't realize."

I shake my head.

"Baby," my mom kneels in front of me, "what just happened? And Adrienne, why the hell you giving my baby weed?"

I break out into tears again, while Adrienne gives them the rundown on my orgasms. She also explains that she thought the weed would help keep me calm and not have an orgasm during the opening. Everyone appears to be genuinely concerned for me. I know that Adrienne is feeling badly about everything, but I'm not going to let her off the hook any time soon.

Chris silently strokes my shoulder and kisses my forehead.

"Ok, Baby, here's what we're gonna do. This fella is going to take you home. Adrienne is gonna get her camera guy and stuff out of here, and Rachel and I are gonna become your stand ins for the evening. And David. Well, he and his arm piece can just do whatever we need done."

I don't speak. Just sniffle and nod my head.

Rachel gives me a hug and tells me she loves me, and that her dad will drop her off at home. David says that if I need anything just call him. He then gives Adrienne a hand up from the floor as my Mom tells Adrienne that she is going have some strong words for her later. Adrienne is smart enough not to respond.

After the room is cleared, Chris tilts my face towards him and simply says, "You could have told me."

I erupt in a new set of tears.

I'm sitting in Dr. Hamilton's office in her comfy leather chair. I have just finished giving her the play by play of the opening night events. I even laugh when I get to the part about sweating under the hot lights and finding out that my bestie had given me a marijuana laced brownie.

"So, how has your first week of business been?" Dr. Hamilton looks even more tan than usual.

"Not bad. There were a few curious folks in the store because of the live feed the first couple of days, but for the most part, there've been a lot of tourists and they don't have a clue. I'm really happy when I'm in the store, and every day, it feels exactly where I am supposed to be."

"And the orgasms?"

"Haven't had one since opening night."

Dr. Hamilton nods and leans back in her chair, "Why do you think that is?"

"Um, I guess one reason is because the store is open. That particular stress has passed. I know running a business won't be easy but I'm going to try to have fun and remember why I wanted my own bookstore in the first place. And um, I started yoga and meditation. It's only been a few days, but I think it will help. And now that everyone important to me knows, I feel more in control, and less like I'm hiding something."

"Good."

"And, well, I got a few emails that helped me put things into perspective. Um, so, I got like three emails from women who recognized what was happening to me and told me that they too have stress orgasms. And even an email from a guy. He said that in college he would spontaneously ejaculate before exams.."

Dr. Hamilton nods, but refrains from commenting.

"So, anyway, it kind of helped me not feel like a freak, even though I know it's not normal."

"Maybe it is normal. For you."

No one can read me or annoy me more than this woman. "Yeah, well, I guess. But I also know that I want to take my body back, so hence the yoga and meditation."

"How are Rachel and your mom handling things?"

"Rachel's fine. She's more concerned about me than she was embarrassed. It definitely has us talking a lot more. About everything. I think she might be starting to see me as a person, and not just her mother. My mom, on the other hand, has probably benefited the most from this mess. Her phone has been ringing off the hook with folks wanting to get the scoop on my 'meltdown' directly from her. And she's happy to oblige. She said it was on the news anyway, so no need to lie about it."

Dr. Hamilton lets out a boisterous laugh. "I would love to meet your mother."

"I'm sure you would love her." I roll my eyes as I say it.

"How are things with you and Adrienne?"

I sigh, "Things are fine. She knows I'm pretty much over it. And I know she feels bad about what happened. I know that she would never intentionally hurt me. She actually thought she was doing a good thing."

Dr. H nods. "And what about Chris?" She tents her fingers and tilts her head down when she looks at me, as if she were wearing glasses and was looking at me over the rim.

"So, Chris stayed with me the night of the incident. He didn't try to make me talk. He just took care of me. It was really nice actually. He slept in my bed and just held me all night. The next morning, he made breakfast for me and Rachel, and we've spoken every day since. We've had platonic dates, and we're taking it slow. Tonight he's taking me out on his boat."

"And how are you feeling about all of that?"

"Actually, it's been great. But I'm ready to move forward."

"What does that mean?"

"It means that I'm ready to see if there is something there between us. I'm meeting him at the marina when I leave here." I then look at my watch and realize that my time is almost up.

"Well, that is interesting. And what about intimacy?"

I'm slow to answer, but decide to be honest. "I'm ready for intimacy. I like him a lot. And ever since he found out about my condition, he's been so supportive. It's nice to have someone focus on me for a change."

"Well, I look forward to hearing more about it at your

next session," she says with a wink. "I'll see you same time next week."

Dr. Hamilton and I stand up simultaneously. She opens her desk drawer and pulls a small box out of it and throws it at me. I catch the box and then laugh when I realize what is inside. A 3-pack of condoms.

I thank her as I head out of her office.

When I reach my car, I drop her box of condoms into my purse next to the box that I had purchased on the way to my session.

I'd tell her next time that great minds think alike.

OUR LITTLE SECRET

ONE

"So, did you finally push Lydia down the elevator shaft? What could make you look so happy this morning?"

"No, that heifer is still on my list." Lydia, Gina's new CFO had been making Eli's life miserable since she revamped their old accounting system. She was trying to make everything lean, and was becoming the bane of Eli's existence. He took a seat on the settee that he had found for Gina's office a couple of years ago in a shop down-town. It was his favorite place to sit. Gina often joked that Eli had purchased it for himself.

"I have finally found a contract IT guy to cover for Kurt while he's out recuperating." Eli looked like he had won the lottery. "And I have your wonderful son to thank."

Gina raised her eyebrows. "Oh, so the guy JJ sent worked out? I'm surprised."

Gina and Eli had tried to offer internships and entry-level positions to a couple of JJ's friends in the past, but things had rarely worked out because the reality of Gina's business often didn't match the students "work as a playground" expectation set by large, national tech companies. When he suggested that Eli interview his friend for the IT contract, Eli agreed only because of his love for JJ, but he had sworn to Gina this would be the last one.

"Work out? Girl, this guy is <u>perfect</u>. He's a little older than I expected, like twenty-eight or nine, but he's mature. He went into the military after high school to pay for college, so he knows how to work in the real world. He's smart, got the kind of experience that we need, and is easy to look at. Whew!" Eli fanned himself with his hand.

"Please tell me this guy can keep the wheels moving until Kurt comes back and that he isn't just pretty to look at?" Gina gave Eli a smirk. She knew that he had a sweet spot for a good looking man.

"He's more than qualified, and has the right skills." He shot her an annoyed look. "And besides, I've got a man at home. Can you say the same?" He laughed at his own words before Gina could even respond.

"Um, ok. We don't have to go there. Thanks for handling this while I prepare to send JJ off into the world. And I don't need a man because I have you."

Eli smiled and cleared his throat as a thoughtful look crossed his face, "You know I'm not going to be here forever. As in here, your right-hand and in the office." He looked uncomfortable, but continued on. "And I think it's time you started grooming someone to take my place. I've been doing a lot of thinking and watching. I think you have a great candidate in house to replace me. You should offer the position to Melissa."

Gina waved her hand to stop Eli from talking. "Look, I know that you and Andre have started the adoption process, but I've still got time, right? Let me just get through JJ's leaving, and then we can talk about it. Next week. I promise."

Eli was the first hire Gina made when she started her company. He managed operations and loved taking on individual projects as well. If Gina had her way, they'd work together until they were old and gray. But she knew that Eli was ready to start a family. She just wasn't ready to lose him.

"I promise," she said again as her office door opened.

Both Gina and Eli turned Lydia as she walked in uninvited. Gina could see the scowl form on Eli's face.

"Sorry to barge in," she said, not sounding sorry at all. "I just need you to sign off on this contract employee that Eli just hired. He sent him to HR to sign all the paperwork, but it didn't have your signature on it." Lydia looked at Eli with a slight smirk.

Gina took a deep breath. Lydia came highly recommended and had a reputation for running a tight financial ship, but they were starting to see that she worked just as hard to be the teacher's pet as she did at her actual job. Gina recognized it for the insecurity that it was. Eli saw it as her attempts to constantly undermine and edge him out.

"Lydia, I've already said that my <u>or</u> Eli's signature is enough to move forward on things. Eli signed off on it, so we're good. This doesn't need my signature. So, please let HR know to move ahead with the contract today.

Lydia looked a bit deflated. "Sure. I'll take care of it. And since the young man is still here, I had Melissa go ahead and start introducing him to the staff. He should be around any minute now."

Lydia let herself out of Gina's office without any additional fanfare.

"I swear 'fore God that one day I'm gonna read her for filth and make her little ass cry." Eli had no problem letting his professional mask slip when he was pissed off.

Gina laughed, "Don't do it, Eli. She's amazing at her job. She just wants to fit in. We were both there trying to prove ourselves at one time. She just needs 'handling'. I'll take care of her."

"You better do it, or I will."

The door to Gina's office opened for a third time before she could respond. She sighed. She was really going to need to put a "knock before entering" sign. Her staff were like kids crashing into their parents bedroom. She usually didn't mind it so much, but today it was feeling a bit extreme.

Melissa, manager of account services, entered with a tall, well-built young man trailing behind her. He wore his hair short, and Gina could swear she could see ripples of muscle through his suit jacket. This was the guy her son recommended? He looked like a grown ass man, not that fresh out of the dorm room guy she was expecting to see. She shot Eli a look. He was right, this guy was easy to look at.

"Uh, Ms. Taylor, this is Michael Thelan. Lydia asked me to show him around and introduce him to the staff. I've already introduced him to everyone else." She stepped aside to let Michael fully enter the room.

Gina stepped from behind her desk and extended her

hand to Michael. He shook with not too firm of a grasp, and before letting go placed his left hand on top of her hand in a move that Gina normally would have considered dominant, but somehow didn't feel that way at all in the moment. In fact, she could swear that she felt a spark of electricity shoot through her hand.

"Thank you so much for giving me this opportunity, Ms. Taylor. JJ talks about you so much, I feel like I kind of know you."

Gina's words stuck in her throat. Good looking, IT smart, and manners. This guy was batting a thousand right now.

"We're happy that you're going to be able to help us out this summer," Eli said, as he sidled up next to Gina. He looked down at their hands, and Gina quickly withdrew hers.

"Yes, uh, yes Michael. Welcome aboard. Eli was just informing me on your contract. He seems impressed, which is a hard thing to do, so kudos to you." Gina looked at Eli with a smile, before continuing. "I look forward to seeing you on Monday. We have a lot we need to do before we roll out our new subscription box in the fall."

"Actually, I'll see you tomorrow," Michael said. "JJ invited me to the graduation party that you're throwing for him."

Gina's face flickered surprised, but then she remembered that JJ had asked to invite a few of his classmates and fraternity brothers, and she'd said the more the merrier.

"Of course. Well, then I'll see you tomorrow night." Her voice sounded a bit high, even to her.

Eli sauntered out of the room behind Michael, but turned back to Gina and mouthed "this dude is hot". Gina did not disagree.

TWO

Young. This guy is young. Too damn young. But boy is he fine. And that chocolate skin of his just made her want to...

"Girl, you betta stop looking at that boy like that. I could tell from the porch that you were getting hot and bothered. I've been watching you watching him."

Gina turned to swat Janette, her best friend, on the arm and then handed her a stack of dishes. "Take these into the kitchen and leave me alone."

"Umm hmm," Janette said, as she accepted the pile and walked away smirking.

Gina had enjoyed the party, but when folks started trickling out to head to their homes, warm beds, or whatever, she couldn't have been happier. She was emotionally and physically drained from the celebration. And if she was honest, she was feeling some type of way about her baby leaving. Not just home, but also the whole country. While he'd traveled abroad before, it was with her or his dad. This was grown man stuff that he was about to embark on. And she wouldn't see him again until Christmas.

Her thoughts continued to bounce around as she cleared the table, until she noticed a flash of white across the yard. As she looked up, she realized that Michael had taken off his shirt, and was about to drag the bags around the side of the yard to the trash cans. She stood and watched as he hoisted the bags as if they were weightless. He then turned and saw her watching him and flashed her a smile so bright, it warmed her insides.

She was rooted to the spot, as he turned the corner to proceed with the trash disposal.

"Um, Mom, can I talk to you for a minute?"

JJ's voice startled her, but she turned to face him.

"Sure, baby, what's up?" She went back to work as he walked over to her.

"I just wanted to let you know that things are going to be taken care of while I'm gone. I don't want you to have to hire someone to cut grass and do chores. I've made arrangements with Michael, and he's going to be available to help you out."

Gina threw her head back and smiled at her son. "Boy, you do realize that I can afford to have someone do chores around my house? Especially now that your dad and I don't have to pony up for your tuition." She chuckled as she spoke. "And anyway, I'm your parent, not vice versa. I look out for myself."

"I know Ma, it's just that I'll feel better knowing that someone I trust is looking out for you. You know Dad never was good with doing anything with his hands, and trust me, I've already asked Michael to check on him too.

I don't know what the two of you would have done without me."

Gina laughed. JJ was right. If something needed fixing or doing at her house or his dad's JJ was the one to handle it. He was five the first time he took one of his toys apart to see what was inside. And when he was done, he put it back together. Everyone thought he would become an engineer, but doing things with his hands was an act of contemplation and relaxation for JJ. James Sr. and Gina learned to appreciate the fruits of their son's labor. Also, it saved her a ton of money on yard work and minor home repairs.

"That's really sweet JJ, but maybe Michael doesn't want to be bothered with your parents. You don't have to worry about me. I got this."

"I know Ma. But he doesn't mind. And like I said, he's gonna check on Dad, too. He helps out his family locally. He's happy to do it."

"I sure am." Gina turned to see Michael standing slightly behind her. Sweat was sitting on his shoulders and glistening in the flood lights he was standing under.

"Well, it seems like the two of you have already decided things." She kept the amusement out of her voice. "Thanks, to both of you for thinking of me."

JJ leaned over and kissed her on the cheek. "I love you, Ma. I just want my girl to be looked after while I'm gone."

"I love you too, now get out of here and go party with your friends so that I can finally put my feet up."

JJ took the remaining mess off the table, and announced that he and his friends were heading out, and that it would probably be a late night.

After the house was empty, and Gina was freshly showered, in bed, and descending into sleep, Michael's sweaty chest and amazing smile popped in her head. Her last waking thought was that she was too old to be fantasizing about some young, hot man.

THREE

Sunday afternoon, Gina wandered into the living room where, JJ had his duffle bag and a ton of clothes spread out on the floor.

"You really need all of that for six months? Where you gonna put it, and how many bags can you carry?"

"No, Mom, I'm not planning to take all these clothes. I actually laid these all out so I can decide what should go. I need things that pair easily, so mostly jeans and shorts, but I need a couple of dressier items as a 'just in case'. But no suit and tie stuff."

"You are such a divo. Your dad marked you good."

"Oh, just Dad? You and your 'never wear cheap shoes or a cheap watch' didn't have anything to do with that?"

Gina laughed. She had to admit that she started drilling certain style and etiquette standards into JJ from the time he turned 12 and became interested in picking out his own clothes. "Boy, don't start with me."

"Uh, huh. That's what you always say when I'm right."

Gina threw a decorative pillow at him that he easily dodged.

"So did you come up with plans for all the things you're gonna do when I'm gone?"

"Nope. No plans. Janette thinks she's the boss of me. Thinks I should use this summer to date like crazy."

"I think she's right."

"What? You want me to date?"

JJ stopped folding a shirt and looked at his mom. "Yeah, actually I do. I think it's time. I don't want you to be alone, and I don't want to worry about you while I'm away."

"You don't need to worry about me. I'm your parent." Gina gave her son a sharp look.

"If I want to worry about you, that's what I'll do. Like it or not, Mom, your kid has grown into a man with opinions separate from yours and the ability to make his own decisions." He looked pointedly at his mother.

Gina held JJ's gaze for a moment, but did not speak. JJ broke the silence by standing up and stepping over his clothes to get to her. He sat next to her on the sofa and grabbed her hand.

"I just want you to enjoy the life you've built. You and Dad gave me a great foundation, but you dote on everyone important in your life. I mean, you even found Dad a wife. Who does that?" He laughed, but pressed on. "Just give yourself some of that time and attention. Go buck wild while I'm gone. Just don't get arrested."

"Uh, Baby, I promise that I'll indulge myself while you're gone, but don't get it twisted, I'm going to miss you like crazy." She reached over and pulled JJ into a hug.

When she let him go she said, "Just make sure you don't come home with anything you didn't leave here with—wives, babies, diseases, none of that!"

JJ shook his head at his mother. "I love you crazy woman."

FOUR

After a week of sneaking glimpses of Michael around the office, but being too busy for direct contact, Gina was awakened on Saturday morning to the sound of the lawn mower. At first she thought it was too early, but when she looked at the clock, she realized that it was 8:00. She couldn't remember the last time she wasn't up and out for a run by 6am on a Saturday morning. Her head was a bit fuzzy from the wine and Netflix binge, but she then remembered that Michael had sent her a text letting her know that he would be cutting the grass this morning. She slowly rolled out of bed, threw on some clothes on and brushed her teeth. She stopped in the kitchen to turned on the Keurig, then headed into the yard to let Michael know she was making coffee.

The lawnmower was sitting in the edge of the back yard, near the gate. As she started toward the side gate, Michael came through with a gas can. He was wearing a sleeveless shirt and a big floppy hat. He was already drenched in sweat.

Michael walked over to her as she shielded her eyes from the sun. "Good morning Ms. Taylor."

Gina tried take her eyes off his broad shoulders. "Good morning, Michael."

"I didn't mean to disturb you. I thought you would be on your run this morning."

"It's no problem. I canceled and decided to sleep in, but the truth is, I wouldn't have slept much longer. My body can't let me rest when the sun is shining. How much longer do you have?"

He pulled a handkerchief out of his back pocket and wiped his brow. "The front is done, and the back will probably take me another 20 minutes if you don't mind me using your riding mower. JJ mentioned it to me before he left."

"You can definitely use the rider. Why did you bring your own mower?"

"I'm heading to my grandmother's when I leave to spend the weekend with her and I usually take care of her yard when I'm there. She doesn't have a mower, and whichever family member that goes to cut her grass brings their own."

"How sweet! Where does your grandmother live?"

"She lives in Manning. I spend the weekend with her every couple of months. She has seventeen grandchildren, and we all pretty much try to spoil her rotten."

Gina nodded, "I tell you what, I'll open the garage so that you can get the rider, and then I'll fix you breakfast for your hard work. I really appreciate the fact that you came over and did this before going to see about your grandmother."

"Thanks Ms. Taylor. I appreciate the offer. Before I

come inside, I'll rinse off the sweat with your garden hose, and change into some fresh clothes in the garage. Hope you don't mind."

Gina's thoughts ran all over the place, as what Michael looked like without any clothes on. She realized that she was slow to answer and pulled herself together.

"That's ridiculous Michael. You can take a shower here, have a decent breakfast, and then hit the road. I'll go open the garage door so you can get to the mower. Just come into the house through the garage when you're done."

"Thanks again Ms. Taylor. A real breakfast sounds great."

"A real meal coming right up. And please call me Gina." She didn't know why she said it, but she just knew that she really wanted him to be less formal with her.

She stood at the window for a moment watching Michael climb on the riding mower to tackle the rest of the yard. She gave herself another minute to appreciate that wide back of his before she turned away from the window and started on the meal.

When Michael came in the kitchen from the garage, everything was done but the eggs. She set the egg carton on the counter and turned to address him. "You can shower and change in the guest room. I'll show you where it is and get you a towel."

"Thanks again. I don't want to put you out."

"It's not a problem."

Michael followed her out of the kitchen and down the hall. While the house was ranch style, it was huge and splayed out. When they reached the guest room, she realized she would need to step aside to let him in. She moved back just as he tried to squeeze behind her. She felt the heat coming off of him as he inadvertently grazed her ass while trying to move past her into the room. She was almost positive that he was going commando within his shorts. She blushed as she stumbled back into the hall and pointed towards the bathroom door.

"Uh, you can use the towels that are hanging in the bathroom. I, um, I have grapefruit, orange, and pomegranate juice." She couldn't keep the embarrassment out of her voice. "Which do you prefer?"

"Orange is fine, Ms, uh, Gina," his smile was warm, yet knowing. He seemed slightly amused.

"Great. See you in a few." Gina couldn't get out of the room and down the hall fast enough. By the time she made it back into the kitchen she was hoping she could get through breakfast without embarrassing herself again.

FIVE

When Michael came into the kitchen a few minutes later, he was wearing a pair of fresh shorts and a dry fit t-shirt. He had thrown on running shoes with no show socks, and his muscles popped in the fitted shirt.

Gina dropped her dish towel on the floor at the sight of him. She remembered her manners and gestured for him to have a seat. The food was ready and she found that even w/out getting in her run that morning, she was starving.

The conversation was polite as they began to dig into their plates.

"You have any siblings?"

"Yep," Michael responded between bites, "a sister. She's my twin. She just moved to Chicago.

"What's it like having a twin?"

He smiled, "We're five minutes apart, but you would think it was ten years the way she's always trying to boss me around."

"So she must be hard on your girlfriend, then." Gina

realized after the words were out of her mouth that the was a lame question.

"She's horrible to women I date, but since I'm not currently dating anyone, no problems there." Michael laughed, and Gina swore she saw a twinkle in his eye.

"OK, so what's up with not dating right now? And don't say because of school. I'm sure you could've managed to do both."

"The girls seem so young. And the women I'm most interested in don't seem to believe that I'm not out here being a 'playa'."

"So what type of women are you interested in?" Gina's eyebrows went up.

"I tend to date women older than I am. That's why my sister gives them such a hard time."

Gina coughed as she choked a little on the orange juice that she had just swallowed.

"You ok?" he asked as he stood up.

She waved at him to sit down, "I'm good. My juice just went down the wrong way." She cleared her throat before she spoke again. "So what is it about older women that you find appealing?"

Michael put his fork down, picked up his napkin, and wiped his mouth. "I like that they already know what they want out of life and who they are. That's sexy to me. Confidence. Self-assuredness. They've already worked through most of their angst and insecurities."

"You seem very wise for someone who's what twenty-seven, twenty-eight?"

"Actually, I'm twenty-nine. I'll be thirty in a few months. And after you've spent eighteen months in Afghanistan putting your life on the line everyday, things kind of take on a different perspective. You spend less time playing and more time filling your life with things that matter."

The mention of JJ was like being splashed with cold water for Gina. She was immediately reminded that she was sitting across the table from one of her son's friends.

As they continued eating and bantering, Gina found that she was impressed with the ease of the conversation and her comfort level with Michael. In fact, she couldn't remember the last time she was so comfortable with anyone but her friends.

Once breakfast was over, Michael began clearing the table and rinsing dishes for the dishwasher. She fell into the rhythm right next to him and loaded the dishes in the machine. She could feel the hair on her arms standing up. If she didn't know better, she would say that he could feel it as well because she caught him giving her lingering looks a couple of times during the clean up. When they were done, Gina folded the dish towel in half and laid it across the sink.

"Thank you again for breakfast Gina," Michael said. "I need to get going or my Gran is gonna blow up my phone wondering where I am or if I've been in an accident. She's big on punctuality."

"You're welcome Michael. I appreciate the yard work. One less thing I'll have to worry about this week."

"No problem. Call me if you need any help with anything around the house. I promised JJ I would look out for you. Seriously, my dad made sure we were all handy around the house. Even the girl." His smile was easy.

"Sounds like your dad is a wise man."

"He likes to think so." They laughed as Michael grabbed his gym bag from by the back door. When he stood, he turned the knob and pulled the door open. "Enjoy your weekend Gina. And don't forget to call me." He gave her one more lingering look, she was sure of it this time, and then he was gone.

SIX

It was Friday and JJ had already been gone for two weeks. Gina had been so busy curating products for the new launch and making sure that they had more than enough inventory that the days flew by. Each day she arrived home exhausted and ready for bed. She loved the feeling of being a maestro and having all the instruments play in harmony. Of course, Eli's planning and monitoring ensured that the trains kept running on time. They were a great team.

During the week, Gina had found that thoughts of Michael would pop into her head during the most random times. First thing in the morning. During her work outs. In the drive thru while she was waiting on her fancy latte. She refused to allow herself to think too long about him. She found that when she fixated on him she became highly aroused. She couldn't believe that she was allowing herself to get worked up over someone so young. She chalked it up to being in a transitional life stage and figured that it would eventually wear off and she'd return to her usual self.

She sat at her desk and listened as the quiet began to descend on the office. It was 5:15 and she should be heading home, but sometimes she liked to stay and just be in her space. As much as she loved the hustle and bustle when her staff was present, she also appreciated the moments when she could sit and reflect on where she was in life.

Gina had taken a chance when she left her VP position at one of the most respected boutique ad agencies in the city. She loved her work, but she craved more. JJ was already a senior in high school and she was thinking about the next steps. She could be home for dinner and attend his basketball games, but she had longed to start something of her own. She wanted to see what she could do with a company that she created from the ground up.

Subscription boxes were becoming a thing. She loved fountain pens and ink and was always on the hunt for a new find. After giving a friend a fancy Japanese fountain pen and ink for a gift, Janette suggested she become a personal shopper for her next venture because she was good at finding the right items for the right person.

Gina mulled over the idea of personal shopping for others and realized that she didn't want to be at someone else's beck and call, but she did love pulling together gift boxes and pens were her specialty. The idea of the Curated Box was born. She did a lot of research before deciding to cash out her retirement fund, at a penalty, of course, to use for seed money. She used social media to create a buzz based on the advice that she had gotten from JJ. She had Eli to thank for the amazing young photographer he brought to the table, and by the time they were ready for launch, they had passed their initial goal for subscribers.

Gina's biggest problem these days was finding hot, new products, so she expanded from just pens and ink to stationery and high end notebooks. It was the best move. She not only could charge more, but she was now being included on lists for luxury good. She kept telling herself that once they got through their fall launch she could slow down for the rest of the year.

Gina was pulled out of her business thoughts when she heard noise in the hall. She looked at the clock and figured that it was probably the cleaning crew coming in to get an early start. That was her signal that it was time for her to go home. She gathered her messenger bag and purse, locked her office, and headed for the elevators. She was looking down at her phone and placing a food order for pick up when she bumped into Michael.

Gina's breath caught in her throat. She had been in product meetings all week, so it had been easy to avoid Michael. Even so, she'd found herself thinking about him and smiling for no reason. She couldn't believe that she was crushing on one of her son's friends. She reminded herself that breakfast had been innocent. Something she would have made for anyone coming over and doing her a favor. So, why couldn't she get the moment of brushing up against him out of her mind? And now, here he was, standing in front of her, smiling and reaching out to catch her from stumbling.

"Hey Gina," Michael said. "So glad to see you. You guys have been keeping me pretty busy this week."

"Uh, yeah, this final push and all." She couldn't

understand why all of a sudden she couldn't make a complete sentence.

"Yeah, well, I'm glad you're still here. I'd love to talk to you about some ideas I have for the roll out. I spoke with Kurt, and he loved them, but he did suggest that I run them by you first. I know it's late, but would you like to have dinner with me? A working dinner, of course." A sexy smile formed on his lips.

"Oh, um, I would love to, but I've already ordered takeout. And I'm pretty tired. But, um, how about you put something on my calendar for Monday, maybe. Book the conference room if you need to." Gina sounded formal, even to herself.

Michael nodded. "Ok, I'll do that. The conference room will work because we can spread out." Gina felt the heat rise in her ace, but simply nodded.

"Well, enjoy your weekend," Michael said when she didn't respond. He stood there smiling at her, but made no effort to head back down the hall or leave.

Gina nodded again, walked to the elevator and pushed the button. The doors opened immediately.

"Well, good night then," she said as she reached to press the button for the ground floor.

Michael reached out and stopped the elevator doors from closing with his hand. "You know, if you need anything this weekend, please don't hesitate to call me."

He flashed her a wide smile, stuffed his hands in his pockets and stood back as the doors started closing. She barely squeaked out an "ok" before they shut.

SEVEN

The computer was frozen. She couldn't open or close a window, and turning it off and then back caused it to open to exactly how she closed it. She was getting frustrated and needed her computer to verify product specs so that she could give the ok on the final list on Monday.

She thought about calling Michael, but figured a call would be awkward. JJ had entered his number into her phone before he left. She was desperate and the Geek Squad couldn't come out until Monday. She took a deep breath and sent the text, hoping that he'd see the message in the next couple of hours. She dropped her phone on the sofa cushion and went into the kitchen to make a cup of tea. She could at least review a couple of reports while she waited.

When she settled on the sofa with her work and tea, she saw the green light flashing in the top left corner of her cell, indicating that she had a message. She was surprised that he responded so quickly.

Michael: Hey Gina, you're not bothering me. I can come over anytime today to look @ your computer.
Gina: That's great. I'm home all day working on a project. What time is good for you?
Michael: How about now?

She hesitated before responding, biting her lip while contemplating how to reply without sounding too eager.

Gina: Now's good.

EIGHT

By the time Michael arrived, Gina had calmed down enough to realize that she was being silly. This young man was coming over to look at and hopefully fix her sluggish computer. Nothing more.

When she opened the door and took in the sight of him in another fitted t-shirt, long gym shorts, and Nikes her rational thoughts were quickly replaced by good old fashioned lust.

"Hey Gina," Michael said as soon as she opened the door.

"Hello Michael". She stepped aside to let him in, while admonishing herself for being so formal. "Thanks for coming over. JJ usually manages my computer stuff, so I really appreciate this.

"No problem." They stood in the foyer for a few seconds before Gina finally snapped to.

"Well, my laptop is in my office. I left it in there in case you need access to the printer and internet stuff."

"Lead the way," Michael said with a smile.

When they got to her office, she explained her issues, and then moved to the sofa to get out of his way. Michael immediately went to work on her laptop. Gina tried to concentrate on the report and spreadsheets in front of her, but she had to keep re-reading and flipping back to pages she had thought she was finished with. She would sneak glimpses of Michael during her page flips. Sexiness and confidence seemed to ooze from him. She could swear that his pheromones were filling the room and making her light headed. And when he finally looked up from her laptop she could not tear her eyes away from him.

"So, you've got some lag because you haven't cleared your cache since, well, ever, it looks like. It was an easy fix. You just need a quick reboot now."

"I don't even know what that means." Gina sputtered. "This thing is only a year old. I thought these newer computers lasted a lot longer." Was she sweating? She was pretty sure she was sweating.

Michael laughed. "It's not a problem really. I'm going to clean some other things up for you. And then I'll show you how you can do it yourself. It'll help your speed return to normal."

"Oh." Gina blinked. "You looked so intent when you were checking things out, I thought it was pretty bad."

"Nah, it's all good. Just wanted to run through your entire system to make sure everything was ok. Plus, I was hoping you'd finish up your work at some point and talk to me."

Gina was caught off guard. "I...Oh...Um."

"It's ok Gina. Your system is fine. I'm actually really glad that you called me. Whatever the reason."

Gina searched his face for humor or amusement. There was none. Before she could respond, he stood up and motioned for her to take her seat at her desk. As she approached him, she was aware that she was beginning to get warm and sweaty. Flushed. When she sat down, he leaned over her to grab the mouse and reposition the keyboard so that he could reach it better. She could smell sandalwood and citrus. Not a cologne, but a lingering soapy, clean smell. She wanted to lean in for a better sniff, but refrained from doing so.

Michael's moves seemed to be slow and deliberate as he showed her how to maneuver through her system to check things herself. His arm brushed up against her and her skin lit up with heat where his skin touched hers. She looked up at him and was shocked to see his eyes burning into her. When he leaned in to kiss her, she didn't pull away. And without thought, she allowed herself to kiss him back.

And wow, could he kiss. The heat in her cheeks spread down her neck and chest, through her belly, and then even further down. The warmth felt delicious and stirred her desire even more. When she realized what was happening, she pulled away. What the hell was she thinking, kissing her son's friend like that. Michael was older than JJ, but not that much older.

Gina did not look at him when she spoke. "Um, we probably shouldn't do this."

"Why not?" He didn't move away. In fact, he seemed poised to resume kissing her at any moment. She sat still because she was unsure of what to do.

"You're a friend of my son's, and you are WAY too young for..." she left the rest of the sentenced unfinished.

"I am JJ's friend, but I am not too young. I told you, I prefer older women. You wouldn't be my first, if that's what you're thinking. I'm attracted to you Gina."

"You're a friend of my son's." Gina knew she was repeating herself, but she felt it needed to be drilled home.

"Well, don't think for a minute that JJ doesn't know about my appreciation for 'older' women."

Gina backed the chair up quickly and got to her feet. "You talked to my son about me?" Her voice was a bit higher than she wanted it to be.

"No. Gina, no! I wouldn't disrespect you or your son like that."

Gina took a deep breath and considered his words. She tried to figure out the best way to take control of the situation. "Why are you telling me all of this? Because of the kiss just now?"

"Look, I've been wanting to kiss you for a while. I feel like we were getting to know each other at breakfast. I enjoyed it and I thought you did, too. I like you, and I'm used to going after what I want."

The tilt of Gina's head and the look on her face told him that he had just hit the wrong note. Gina quickly recovered from her unease. "So, I'm a challenge? A new target to hit?"

"No Gina. You aren't. You're sexy, fun, and interesting as hell. And I'd like to spend some time getting to know you better. I have no games to play. Just one grown up liking what he sees in another grown up."

Gina held in the laugh as he referred to himself as a grown up, but he could see it in her eyes. "Oh, I see Gina. Well, I'll tell you what, when you're ready to deal with me as a grown man and get to know me a little bit better, give me a call. He then leaned down and kissed her again. Slowly and deeply while cupping her face. Afterwards, he stepped back and said, "I'll show myself out. But I do hope you'll call."

NINE

Gina managed to get dressed and head out for Sunday brunch with Janette at The Granary, barely having a thought about what happened between her and Michael the day before. She was on the fence about telling Janette because her best friend had lots of opinions about everything. Until Gina sorted things out for herself, she would forgo8 hearing what Janette thought.

"So with JJ gone for the next few months, will you finally put yourself back out there and start dating again?" Janette asked as soon as the mimosas were on the table.

Gina sipped her drink slowly, and then shrugged her shoulders. "Girl, I don't even know where to start. I feel like I've been out of the game a long time."

"You dated after you and James broke up."

"Barely. Then JJ was in the middle of full blown teen angst, and it was enough trying to keep him focused and on track."

"I think you should get on Tinder or Bumble or Match. A lot of folks are finding their husbands there."

"I am not looking for a husband, Chile. I just want to go on a few dates, have some great conversation, and if I'm lucky, I'll find someone to have some great sex with. But I'm not interested in a 'dating mill'. I just want to do me with someone who gets me."

"I hear you. You know marriage isn't on my list of things to do either. But I don't plan to be alone for the rest of my life. Eventually, I'm going to find a companion to live out my days with, but until then, I'm going to have some fun. And that's what I want for you. Fun. You do remember fun, don't you?"

"Ha ha, Janette. Yes, I remember fun. But I also know that you can't force a good fit. And the guys I know just aren't that interesting."

"Let's face it, you don't know that many guys. And no, the ones you know aren't that interesting."

"I'd tell you to back up off me, but there you go speaking that truth again."

The food arrived, and conversation became minimal as they enjoyed their meal. By the time they decided to split dessert, Janette was back on the subject of Gina and her lack of dating the last few years. "Look Gina, it is beyond time for you to put yourself first. JJ is an amazing young man, but your day-to-day work as a parent is done. He's off experiencing life, and you need to remember that you deserve a life."

"I have a life Janette. It may not look like yours, but it's a good one, nonetheless. Shit, I even have a friendship with my ex and his wife. Tell me how many people you know that can actually say that."

"Girl, you love you some Cathy. I think if he messes things up with her, you'll scoop her up."

"Ha! Ok, you may be right on that one, especially since I'm the one that introduced them."

"Yeah, I still can't believe you found your ex-husband a wife. Who does that?" Janette laughed.

"We're unconventional, but it works. And I have the best sidekick for life that a person could ask for. You are really my soul mate. I have all I need."

"Well, now it's time for you to get a few things you want. Like an ass tightening orgasm. Companionship is natural. We weren't meant to be alone."

"Really, Janette? This is coming from you? The woman who has sworn to never get married because marriage holds not benefit for women. Am I hearing you right?"

"Hey, marriage may not be for me, but that doesn't mean it's not for you. I made my choices long ago, and I really believe they're best for me. Girl, you're a woman who functions best in a relationship. You miss throwing couple dinner parties, and couples Halloween outfits, and shit like that. I'm your bestie. You can't hide from me."

"Ugh, if you were talking about me three to five years ago, I would say 'hell yeah, I want that again'. But these days, I really do miss the physical more than anything. I have peace, but I do want to lean on broad shoulders and fall asleep after he's blown my back out." Gina smiled wickedly at Janette.

"Say what now? What do you know about getting your back blown out? And I'm not even sure the kids are still calling it that, so don't say that in public!" Janette stage whispered.

"I'm just saying Janette, don't think I don't have needs. I've just been taking care of business myself. And it's so boring! There is only so much soft porn you can watch, cause the hard stuff is really not my cup of tea, and my imagination is boring me as well. I'm middle aged, not dead, honey."

"Hmph, well, I say you take a page out of the Male Playbook. Find you some young thing to get on top of. Or under. However you like it. They have fewer back problems."

"I don't want anybody I need to teach. If you don't know what you're doing, school is not in session here."

"I'on know girl. You might want to rethink that. Teaching them to give you exactly what you want isn't necessarily a bad thing."

"True. Let's toast to that." They raised glasses and toasted. "But really Janette, what do I look like messing around with a young man?"

"Satisfied. Your ass would look satisfied."

TEN

Gina moved through her workdays with tiny flashbacks of the kiss, causing her to smile unexpectedly. She replayed his words over and over, looking for the lie, dishonesty, or just a young man running game. But her gut told her there was none of that. The situation was what it was.

Michael had indeed scheduled a meeting on Monday in the conference room. He walked her through the work that he had done, and had even included Kurt via video chat. He was responsible, efficient, and bright. Any company would be lucky to have him. According to Kurt's latest check in, he would be back in a couple of weeks, so Gina knew that her time with Michael wasn't long.

When Eli invited her to hang out with him and Andre at Spectators, the fancy sports bar near her house to watch Game 1 of the NBA finals on Thursday, she took him up on the offer.

At the last minute, she used her app to schedule a ride to Spectators so that she could drink and let her hair down. It had been a long week, and since she had gotten her a large portion of her project wrapped up early, in spite of her distractions, she was pretty sure coasting was on the agenda for her at work the next day. She changed into jeans and a fitted Milwaukee Bucks short sleeve shirt, while penny loafers with no socks finished the outfit. She pulled her hair into a high puff, put on her hoop earrings, and freshened up her lipstick. She was stuffing her house keys, ID, and credit cards into her small crossbody bag when she got the notification that her ride was outside.

Eli and Andre were already posted up at a large round pub table in the middle of the bar when she walked in. A lemon drop martini and mild buffalo wings waiting on the table for her. They had arrived early to spend some time alone and catch up since Andre had just gotten back from Italy a couple of days earlier. Andre was an obstetrician and he'd given a presentation at a conference. They had been together for over six years, and Eli liked to travel with him when he could, but he skipped this trip due to the upcoming launch. Eli had a lemon drop martini and mild buffalo wings waiting on the table for her. She double kissed them both and climbed into the high bar chair.

"Hey fellas! Good looking out with the waiting food and drinks. This is why you'll always be my work husband Eli." They raised a toast and Gina noticed the two men exchange a look. She waited until she put her glass down to ask what was up.

Eli held her gaze and then Andre rubbed his shoulder. "Gina, I'm not going to be your work husband for too much longer."

"What? Why?" Gina's questions came out in a shriek.

"It's happening. We're getting a baby. I wanted to tell you a couple of weeks ago, but I didn't want to jinx it. But it's really happening this time. We're getting a baby! Finally!" His eyes were brimming with excitement.

Gina reached over and grabbed Eli's hand as tears began to form. "I'm so happy for you. I really am! But I'm also going to miss seeing you daily. No one has had my back like you. I can't believe you guys are really starting your family."

"Ugh, are you two done yet? You'll always be together. And we live fifteen minutes away. Eli is gonna call you every time the baby cries. And you're going to answer." Andre got up and hugged her from behind and then kissed her cheek. "Now, can we eat, because the game is about to start, and I can't have y'all in here yelling with food in your mouths. Lebron needs to show little Curry what he's working with. <u>Again</u>."

Eli gave Andre the side eye. "Dude, you're too pretty and too smart to live in such a fantasy land."

Gina finished off her first drink and ordered another one. Losing Eli was going to be hard, and having to groom Melissa meant that she was going to have a major shift in her work life, which she was not ready to deal with. It suddenly felt like everything was changing around her with JJ gone, and she was not able to stop it. By her third drink, she was glad that she had not driven her car. And that thought had her ordering her next drink.

She was coming back from the ladies room during halftime when someone called her name and then reached out and touched her arm. She jumped and turned around only to come face to face with Michael.

"What're you doing here?" She was too tipsy to bother with pleasantries.

"I'm here watching the game with some friends. I saw you head to the restroom. Didn't mean to startle you." Michael started walking with Gina back to her table. Eli and Andre shared a look when they arrived.

"Hey Michael," Eli said, "how 'bout you join us for the rest of this game. My husband is a Lebron fan, so you have been warned."

Michael looked at Gina. "You don't mind do, do you?"

Gina tried to appear nonplussed with her shrug. "Nah, unless you're dumping some friends, or a date." She looked around, but there didn't seem to be any woman waiting for Michael's return.

"No, I'm here with a couple of frat brothers, but they won't miss me for a while."

"Then it's settled. Join us." Eli said, patting the empty chair to his right.

Gina decided now would be a good time to switch from martinis to water because a clear head around Michael would be in her best interest. As the Warriors and the Cavaliers battled it out, there was lots of light banter and trash talking. Gina found that in spite of the happy/sad note that the night started on she was having a good time.

At the start of the 4th quarter, Andre's cell went off. Eli was the first to notice the vibrating phone as it moved around the table. "Looks like somebody's baby is ready to make an appearance." After reading the message, Andre made his apologies as he prepared to leave.

"Eli, you can stay babe. I'm sure you and Gina want to taunt Michael for the last quarter."

"No, I know the Warriors are going to finish this off. I'll go home and get some sleep. You good Gina?"

"I'll make sure she gets home." Michael chimed in before Gina could answer.

Eli raised his eyebrows, but Gina gave him a nod. He and Andre shook hands with Michael and kissed Gina before they left.

As they sat through a commercial, Michael turned to Gina and said, "I owe you an apology for the kiss on Saturday. I should never have kissed you without your permission. I promise, I do it again. Unless you want me to." His eyes twinkled as he spoke. Or they were catching the light from all the televisions around them. She couldn't be sure. And maybe she was still a little drunk because instead of answering him, she leaned over and kissed him. Gently at first, and then with full on tongue.

"How about you make sure I get home. Right now."

Michael stood and handed her her purse. She accepted it and took his hand as he led her out of the bar.

ELEVEN

They talked about the game and whether or not the series would go to seven games on the drive to her house. She used the conversation to take her mind off the sexiness that was coming at her in waves. She felt like she was being overpowered by his presence. He insisted on walking her to the door, and once unlocked, she pulled him inside and began kissing him while standing in her foyer. He pulled her tightly to him, and gave in to the kiss. His lips were soft and his kissing was more sensual than intense. Just when she thought she would float away from the goodness of it all, Michael stopped kissing her and pulled back.

"I need you to be comfortable with this. And anything that may come next." The timbre from his voice vibrated through her.

She stepped out of her loafers and pulled him across the room to her couch. "I'm comfortable with all of this." She sat down, pulled him down next to her, and then straddled him. His hands gripped her ass as he leaned back and pulled her tight. Gina could feel him harden and grow beneath her. He slid his hands under her shirt and alternately rubbed her lower back and dipped his hands into her pants. She began to grind into him as the heat from his hands kicked her arousal into high gear.

Gina was relishing the kissing and the fact that she felt like a teenager whose parents weren't at home. But her rational side kicked in and started to make a list of all the reasons she shouldn't let things go any further. Those thoughts began to fall away when Michael lifted her shirt over her head. She didn't take her eyes away from his face, as he unhooked her bra and set her breasts free. She watched him watch her, but gasped with the pleasure of his warm hands when he caressed her breasts and began to circle her nipples with his thumbs. She started melting under his touch, and all she wanted to do is put her lips back on his. But that was not to happen.

"Gina, we can stop at any time. Just say the word. I don't want you to ever feel uncomfortable with me."

Her head was fuzzy from the alcohol and reeling from the sensation of his hands on her body. She leaned in to continue kissing him, but he pulled back.

"I'm serious Gina. You have to tell me what you want every step of the way."

Gina wanted him to keep kissing her and more. So much more. But it looked like he wasn't planning to move forward until she gave him the all clear. "Look Michael, I'm not stuck in last week. I know I may have reacted harshly, it's just that whether we talk about it or not, there is this huge age gap, and well, folks can't find out about this, especially JJ. No one can know about any of this."

"It can be our little secret Gina. That's not a problem." His grin was devilish and hot.

"Well, let's start with no more talking." Gina attempted to push Michael back down, but instead he gently lifted her off of him and moved her to the couch. He leaned her back against the armrest and stretched her legs out down the length of the couch. He then bent down and started sucking and licking her right nipple. She caressed his head as she allowed herself to enjoy the sensations that were shooting throughout her body. It had been eight months since she had a casual fling with someone she met at a product trade show. She had later laughed about it with Janette and Eli. She'd told them how it had been so rote and boring. Nothing like how Michael was making her feel now.

"What don't you want me to talk about Gina? How you like it when I do this?" Michael flicked his tongue across her nipple, and she felt electricity shoot through her. "Or when I do this?" He flicked her other nipple and she thought she would go insane. Instead, she moaned just a little. "You don't want anyone to know how much you like this?" His voice was soft and low in her ear. She wanted to press against his rock hard dick and was rewarded with his hands kneading her ass and pulling her against him. His bulge bumped her clit, just enough to make her jerk. It was exactly what he wanted.

With a grin, Michael slowly watched her as his hands moved to the front of her pants. He found the button on her jeans and popped them open without fanfare and without breaking his stare. She was getting hotter just watching him watch her. Once her jeans were unzipped, he slowly began to pull them down, catching her panties on the side so that they would come down as well. For a fraction of a second, Gina considered stopping him in his tracks, but he was so damn sexy and so damn intense. She wanted whatever he was serving, so she lifted her hips from the couch to make it easier. His grin turned into an amazing smile, and she knew that there was no going back for her tonight.

Once her jeans were off and on the floor, Michael gently parted her legs and began to caress her clit with his thumb. He watched her squirm and close her eyes. She wanted to feel and experience everything that he was offering her, and she didn't want her sight to inhibit the experience.

She cried out when she found that Michael's tongue had replaced his thumb. He began licking and sucking and circling her clitoris like it was his job. Michael controlled the rhythm of her body. He made her respond faster and slower, just by changing the speed of his tasting. Just when she thought she would explode with him sucking on her clit, he would ease up and lick her lightly. Giving her time to catch her breath. At one point she reached for him to pull him up, and let him know that she was ready to give him more, but he grabbed her hands and held them over her head with one hand. He looked up at her and grinned again.

"It's time."

Before Gina could ask "time for what?" he resumed his gentle sucking. Then he rolled his tongue along her clit in a way that had her inching backwards. He chased her with his tongue and then found her slick, wet vagina with his finger. Gina couldn't focus on breaking contact because the heat was blooming from the inside out. As Michael matched the rhythm of his finger with his tongue, sounds began to escape Gina that surprised even her. As her hips pushed into his face, he stopped licking and finished her off by sucking on her as if she was giving him the milk of life. Gina's shudder was deep. Her hips again rose off the couch as her anus tightened with a pleasure of its own. She had never come so hard that her ass had tightened up.

As she lay there feeling not just the heat recede from her body, but also as if she had released something amazing into the universe, Michael got up and headed down the hall. She tried to lift her head to ask him where she was going, but she couldn't and didn't want to move. If he was going to tie her up, now would be the best time to do it because she her body was jelly.

Michael with a bottle of water and her robe. She politely accepted, his eyes never leaving her face as she slipped on the robe.

"Um, I'm not sure what I need to say right now," Gina started to speak.

Michael put his own water bottle down and pulled her to him as he sat down. She ended up on his lap. He slowly started kissing her gently. She wasn't sure if the kiss was making her dizzy or the alcohol, but either way, she liked it. When he finally stopped, he cupped her face and then kissed her cheek.

"I'm going to go home now. I had a really good time tonight. I want to see you again, so I plan to call you tomorrow."

Gina took a deep breath, and merely nodded. She

didn't want to talk and break the sexy spell. Michael gently placed her on her feet and lead her to the door.

"See you in the morning, Gina", he said before he opened the door, "I'm looking forward to showing you what else I can do."

TWELVE

The buzz of her cell phone pulled her out of her office daydream about the night before. She started getting back to back messages. Janette and then Michael.

The girlfriends wanted to know what was up and why didn't she call or text anyone last night. And Michael wanted to know if she was free for dinner. She knew she needed to respond, but she wasn't ready to have the "guess what I did" conversation with Janette yet. And she was pretty sure what Michael had planned for dinner, but she wasn't so sure that she was ready to be on the menu. Again.

As she was making up her mind to respond after lunch, Eli walked in with a silly grin on his face.

"So you gonna spill the beans or what?" Gina blinked up at him, opened her mouth and then closed it again. What the hell was she going to say about last night? Should she say anything about last night? She decided that keeping last night to herself was her best bet right now.

"No beans to spill. Michael took me home, made sure I was safe, and then he went home."

Eli raised his eyebrows at her. "Really? That's it, huh? Nothing happened?"

Gina could feel the flush rising. She had to stay chill. She really never could put anything over on Eli. She needed to convince him, or he wasn't going to stop until she was telling him all the sordid details.

"Eli, really, he made sure I got in the house, cause I was a bit tipsy, and then he went home. The guy is a gentleman. There was no funny business. Not that I don't think he is a true hottie, but come on, he's JJ's friend. Plus, he's a contractor for my company. It wouldn't be a good thing to do." Throwing in a bit of truth always helped the lie go down a little smoother. And obviously, Eli bought it, because he smirked at her and replied, "Yes indeed Girl, that young'un is <u>hot</u>!"

They both laughed and Gina felt relief wash over her. She knew she wasn't out of the hole, but at least Eli was happy that she gave him a little dish. For now.

"So, other than to see if you got laid by the PYT, I came in to see what your plans are for the weekend."

"No plans right now, why?"

"Andre and I are hosting brunch. Kind of a celebration thing. I still feel horrible about breaking the news to you. Have you spoken to Melissa yet?"

"No, not yet. She's been out in meetings but we have our usual review hour this afternoon." Gina spun a pen on her desk as she spoke.

"Can I be there when you tell her she's getting a promotion? I want to see her face. She definitely deserves it."

"You can, but I will still miss you like crazy. No matter how great Melissa is."

"Girl! You and me? Us never part!"

"Get out of my office Eli", Gina said with a laugh. Once he started quoting The Color Purple, it was all over.

Eli came around her desk, stood her up and gave her a hug. "Seriously Girl. We family." Gina hugged him back, and then pushed him away. Her phone was going off again, and she didn't want Eli to see if the message was from Michael.

"I love you, too, now get out so I can get some work done."

As soon as Eli was out the door she picked up her phone.

Michael: *How about dinner at my place?*

She drummed her fingers on the desk as she thought about what she should do. Finally, she tapped out:

Gina: *What's the address and what time?*

She knew when she hit send that she was in trouble.

THIRTEEN

Michael rented a bungalow on the property of a young Charleston power couple. It had its own driveway and she pulled up behind his car. She held the bottle of wine in one hand and rang the doorbell with the other. She was surprised by how quickly Michael opened the door. She thrust the bottle at him and said "Hey! I brought wine." Oh my God, she thought. What the hell is wrong with me?

Michael laughed, said hello, and grabbed the bottle of wine. He then leaned in to give her a hug, and she became overwhelmed by the fresh smell of him. He was wearing jeans, a t-shirt, and was barefoot. He looked so relaxed that she immediately began to feel a bit more at ease around him.

"Come in Gina. Welcome to my home." He took the bottle from her and planted a kiss on her cheek.

In the kitchen he began grabbing glasses and rummaging for a wine cork, while Gina stayed in the living room. She took notice of the obligatory Big Ass Man TV, but also noticed that he had stacks and stacks of books on the floor. He had a couple of floating book-shelves that were full, and more books stacked next to the sofa. She was immediately endeared. A man after her own heart. She began looking at the titles and easily spotted the trends. Michael liked sports biographies, sci fi, philosophy, and photography. Damn. When she saw the bookshelf full of black writers, fiction and nonfiction, she was really impressed.

"You like my books?", he asked as he handed her a glass of wine.

"I do. Have you read them all?"

He looked insulted. "Of course. I've got more in the guest room and the bedroom. My parents didn't play when it came to reading or education."

"I wasn't trying to imply anything. It's just that reading seems to be somewhat of a lost art for folks these days. I'm just super excited when I come across another bibliophile."

"Well, you'll have to suggest some titles to me. Read-ing's one of my favorite ways to lose track of time." He smirked as he led her to the big oversized chair that sat directly facing the television. She noticed the he took the couch, but she didn't say anything.

"I'd love to, but right now, all I can focus on is the wonderful smell coming from your kitchen. What are you cooking?" As if to prove that she wasn't lying, her stomach let out a loud rumble.

"Ahh, well, I'm cooking Cornish hens, roasted broc-coli and Brussel sprouts and sweet potatoes. I hope you like it. I'm a good cook, if I do say so myself."

"So, I'll be the judge of you being a good cook, cause I'm a great eater. If I do say so myself." The smile and laugh that came out of Gina was genuine and easy. She felt so comfortable with this man.

"You cook, you're a voracious reader, you're handy around the house. You have to have a weakness somewhere."

"I do, I have a weakness for smart, sexy women." He looked directly at her and held her gaze.

She dropped her eyes and reached for her glass, but then recovered quickly. "Well, I have a thing for a great meal, so don't let dinner burn."

And dinner was wonderful. Gina had not tasted anything so good in a long time. While Michael was no slouch in the kitchen, he swore that he couldn't bake "for shit", so he produced a couple of slices of cookie pie that he copped from Kaminsky's earlier that day. He warmed them, added two healthy scoops of fancy vanilla ice cream, and served dessert to Gina in the living room. She was as full as a tick, but that did not stop her from eating every last bite. She knew that her run tomorrow was going to be slow and torturous.

When Gina stepped out onto the patio she was not prepared for the pool and jacuzzi, which was bubbling with alternating flashing lights. It was early June, but the evening still had a slight chill. This would only last for another week or so, so she didn't mind sitting outside and enjoying the breeze. She took up residence on super cushiony lounge chair, took her shoes off and stretched out. Michael settled in on the chair beside her.

They were close enough to touch, and she was slightly surprised when he reached over and grabbed her hand. He caressed her fingers, while lying back looking up at the moon. Gina said nothing and just enjoyed the touch. It was quiet and comfortable, and she was feeling on the verge of going into a food and wine coma. She was sleepy, relaxed, and content.

Michael rolled over to face her and brought her hand to his mouth. He quietly mumbled, "I want you Gina. I have been feeling you for a while. And now I want to feel you."

She didn't turn to look at him. She didn't want him to see that she was feeling the same way. She couldn't blame it all on the food and drink, but she knew that her defenses were down and it would be hard to resist him. Whatever his age, he had showed her over the last week or so that he really was a grown ass man. And she was a grown ass woman. She could do what she wanted with whomever she wanted. But she knew it wasn't that easy.

"Michael, I'm not sure about this. I mean, I really like you, and if I'm honest, you could have my head spinning, but this thing would be too close for comfort, if you know what I mean."

"Gina, you don't seem like a woman who is bound by other people's opinions of you. I'm saying, if you like me and want to use me, you can do that. I'm here for your pleasure." He didn't blink and he didn't smile. His seriousness caught her off guard.

"I am not trying to do relationships or complications, Michael."

"Who said anything about relationships or complications? I'm saying that I would like to do some very adult things with a woman that I am extremely attracted to, and I hope that she will want to do those adult things with me too. Tonight. I don't have any thoughts beyond tonight. Well, maybe tomorrow night as well because all I have planned for this weekend is waiting to hear if I've got this cyber security job in Austin that starts next month. So yeah, help me take my mind off the long wait."

His grin was devilish, and she couldn't help but smile back at him. <u>What could be the harm</u>, she thought to herself. She would, at the very least, spend time with an intriguing man.

He could see that she was thinking about his proposal, so he thought he'd give her a little something to think about. Michael sat up, took his shirt off, leaned over to kiss Gina gently and slowly, and then stood up, walked towards the pool and turned around to face her. He slowly unbuckled his jeans, eased his jeans down, and stepped out of them. He was definitely putting on a show for her Gina had been surprised to see that he had been commando all night. But what really captured his attention was the way his penis began to become erect, and point right at her. Damn, that thing was something to look at. The twitch that hit her vagina let her know that Miss Kitty was in agreement.

"The water is warm. Feel free to join me." He turned and jumped in, submerged himself, and once he came up, began to swim to the deep end. Once there, he turned and looked at Gina and swam back. "You coming in or nah?"

"What about the home owners?" Gina asked, looking back towards the house.

"Gone for a long weekend."

Gina hesitated for a moment, then stood up and took her top off. She then stepped out of her own jeans. As she stood in her bra and panties, she asked herself what she was doing, but then Miss Kitty shut that shit down with a quickness as Michael started floating on his back with his dick in the air. She unsnapped her bra and dropped her panties and walked down the steps into the pool. She was thankful that he was not lying about the pool being warm because her nipples were tight and taut thanks to the slight breeze that just blew. And that damn mighty fine penis of his. Man, if he couldn't fuck, she was going to be mad as hell.

They swam, kissed and played. Gina found herself leaning against the side of the pool looking up at the moon and wondering when was the last time she let her hair down like this. She couldn't remember. And while that made her sad, she vowed to make sure that she let herself live more. Whatever that looked like.

"Penny for your thoughts," Michael said as he came up behind her.

"You can have them for free," Gina said without turning around. "I was just enjoying being in the moment here with you. Sometimes I need to remember to stop and just be. That is what I'm doing tonight, so thank you."

Michael wrapped his arm around her waist and began kissing her shoulders and along her neck. "Thank you for sharing that." His dick pressed against the back of her thigh, and she pressed back against it. She felt it harden and jump as it inched up along her buttocks. Without thinking, she shifted and pressed her butt harder against him.

They stood like that for several moments before Gina wrapped herself around him. She embraced him and began kissing him deeply and intensely, letting him know what she wanted from him.

"If you have condoms, take me to your bed. If you don't, I guess you'll have to miss out on all of this." She resumed kissing and grinding him.

His voice was a bit of low growl in her ear, "Woman, I've got condoms, but don't play with me. You gotta say you want this."

She leaned forward to kiss him again, but gently bit his lip instead. "I want this".

No other words were exchanged as Michael led her out of the pool past the discarded clothes, into the house, and down the hall into his room. He opened the bathroom door and pulled a couple of large fluffy towels out and tossed them onto the bed instead of handing them to her.

"Um, you're not going to dry me off?" Gina asked as she turned to reach for a towel.

"Nope. I want you cold and wet. That way you won't cum too fast."

"That sure of yourself, huh?" Gina tweaked his nipples with her thumbs and forefingers and his dick jumped.

"I am." He backed Gina up to the bed, until she fell back unceremoniously on the towels. He then reached into his nightstand drawer and took out a condom. She watched him remove it from the package and roll it on his still hard dick, biting her bottom lip in anticipation.

As she scooted back on the bed and got ready for him to enter her, she realized that he was moving slowly. She thought he was trying to give her time to change her mind, so she grabbed at the base of his penis and began to guide him into her. He put his hand out to stop her.

"I got this woman."

That turned her on even more.

Michael didn't rush his game. In fact, by the time he got the tip of his penis inside, Gina was greedy for more and trying to pull him into her. He gave her his tongue in her mouth instead while inching his way in. He could see her desire, and he wanted to keep that look on her face for just a bit more.

But torturing Gina was also torture for himself. He finally gave in and gave her the full length of his cock. While she made no sound, the arch of her back told him everything he needed to know. For the next few minutes, he gave her the slow stroke. Slowly in, slowly out, all rhythm and intensity, pushing against her clit when he hit the top. He knew he had found her spot when he could no longer slow her down. She became a force to be reckoned with, and when she commanded that he roll over, he did as he was told.

Once in the dominant position, Gina began to rock and buck into Michael with abandon. But once she settled him in deep and began to do a short but intense bounce, he could only hope to hold on and let her release first. When she leaned into him and held his chin with her hand, he knew it was over. She was about to explode and she wanted to make sure that he was watching her. And once her pussy began to rhythmically tighten around him, he began his own release.

She lay down on top of him and let the chlorinated

water and the sweat from each of their bodies commingle. She didn't remember feeling him go soft or rolling off of him. Instead, she just slipped into a blissful nap.

FOURTEEN

Saturday was pretty quiet for Gina with some texting between her Michael. She really just took the day to relax, read, and eat. The week had been such a roller-coaster for her, the slow relaxing day felt like a treat, and she wanted to relish in the deliciousness of the night before. By the end of the day, she received a text from Michael:

Michael: *Got the call I was waiting on this afternoon. New cyber security gig in Austin with Jensen Tech. They want me to start as soon as I wrap up with you guys. Can I swing by to celebrate?*

Gina was excited about his news. She was happy for him. And she was happy about the time they'd spent together. Maybe they could ride the last couple of weeks out and continue to enjoy each other. No strings.

Gina: *Sure, how about a short hike in Awendaw tomorrow* *morning, before brunch. I need the exercise since I missed my run this morning and haven't done anything all day. Meet at my house at 7:30.*

Michael: *Cool.*

Her cell rang just as she closed out the message app on her phone. It was Janette.

"Hey girl," Gina said, a little too upbeat.

"Don't 'hey girl' me! I haven't talked to you since Wednesday. It's Saturday. And don't think your damn text messages are ok. That was just enough to let me know your ass was still alive." Gina waited for Janette to catch her breath.

"Are you finished?"

"No. I'm just getting started. What have you been up to? I hope you haven't been sitting home depressed and feeling sorry for yourself because JJ is gone."

"I am not feeling sorry for myself Janette. I've been busy."

"Doing what?"

"Um, I don't know. Stuff. I hung out with Eli and Andre the other night at Spectators. Work. Stuff. You haven't been by here to see if I was dead or not, so please stop with all the drama."

"Actually, Gina, I came by last night. You weren't home."

"Oh. Uh, what time was that? I had dinner with a potential client. They were cool. We ended up talking for a long time."

"When did you start having client dinners on a Friday night?"

"When that's the only time my client can meet Janette!" Gina feigned frustration. "Look I'm home now. Chilling. And that is what I intend to do for the rest of the weekend."

"You are going to Eli's brunch tomorrow, right?" Janette asked. "I'm going to go a little early because I promised him I'd bring some extra serving dishes.

"Of course I am. 12:30 right?"

"Yes, Gina. And don't be late. Eli is not a happy camper when his productions don't go off as planned. But you know this already."

"I'll be there. On time. And looking good. You don't have to worry about me. Now can I go back to enjoying my quiet time? I promise we'll catch up tomorrow. You good? And can you save some of the fussing for tomorrow?"

"Don't be so snippy! I'm good. Plus, I need some of that chill time myself. See you tomorrow, girl."

Gina hung up the phone and sunk deeper into the sofa. She should have told Janette about Michael, but she figured, he was leaving soon. She could tell her after he was gone. She was enjoying keeping things under wraps. Michael was simply a gift that she had given herself. She couldn't think of the last time she'd done something without considering someone else. And with Eli leaving sooner rather than later, it was a great way to release stress.

FIFTEEN

Michael rang her doorbell at exactly 7:30. He had on workout gear, a ball cap, and sunglasses. As soon as she opened the door, she saw that he was carrying a bag and two cups of coffee. Before she could take the bag from him, he leaned in and kissed her. In the open. In her doorway.

She pulled him inside, and shut the door. And then she kissed him back, finally breaking away to acknowledge his offering.

"Whatever is in the bag, thanks so much. I was gonna eat a banana and drink a bottle of water before we headed out."

"Well, I figured you would need fuel for the hike, and whatever comes after." He raised his eyebrows and smiled at her. "Or should I say for when you cum after? Either way, I got you a sausage biscuit and a vanilla latte."

Lord, this guy just oozed sexy. She started to get all warm and tingly just hearing his words. She could honestly say that she had enjoyed the last few days with him. She just wasn't going to tell him that right now.

"Well, it's still a 20 minute drive here, so how about we eat in the car? We can take my Jeep since I know the way, and I packed the bug spray, sunscreen, and extra water last night."

"I'm good with that. Or we could stay in bed and I can provide a workout of a different nature." He pinned her against the wall and began to kiss her and grind his rising erection into her. "Cause these running pants you got on are turning me on."

"So," Gina said as he continued kissing her, "let's make a deal. Um, we get out and get some exercise and sunshine for an hour for me, and then we come back and see how many ways I can fuck you for an hour before I have to get ready for brunch at Eli's. Besides, I want to hear about your new gig." She gave his tight ass a squeeze for emphasis.

"You are a tough negotiator, Gina. I'll take you up on that offer."

By the time they had made it to the Awendaw Passage, Gina knew all about his new job. The perks, benefits, and salary were impressive. This guy was not going to be anyone's broke millennial.

Austin was one of her favorite cities, and though she hadn't been in a couple of years, she was able to suggest some sights to see, and of course, she was pretty sure that 6th Street hadn't changed much. As she listened to his plans, she felt excitement for him. He was about to start a career that he would hopefully enjoy for a long while. It was just a reminder of how young and fresh he was.

Since Gina had a full day ahead of her, she decided to do a three mile loop. Enough to get her blood pumping, but not too long that she would be late for brunch. Of course, Michael had no problem with the hike. They talked so much that Gina was caught off guard when they rolled back up on the parking area. It had taken them just about an hour. She was happy that she had been fully prepared with the bug spray and sunscreen, but the heat and humidity was a bit more than she thought it would be. So much for a mild June.

By the time they reached her house, all she wanted was a cold drink and a shower. She decided that she could do both. They left their shoes in the garage, and then headed into the kitchen, where Gina retrieved a cold pitcher of sweet tea of out the fridge and glasses out of the cabinet and put them on a tray. Michael headed for her bedroom. He marveled at the size of her bathroom and luxury shower as he waited for Gina.

The gray tiles on the floor were so light, they almost looked white, but they complemented the porcelain slabs on the walls of the shower. There was a clawfoot tub under the window, but it was the shower stall itself that was a thing of beauty. She had four sprayers on opposite walls and a rainfall shower head dropping down from the middle of the ceiling. The space was large enough to fit four large linebackers, and had a bench along the longest wall.

Michael let out a low whistle. "Damn, Gina, I guess you take your bathrooms seriously."

Gina laughed. "Yeah, I do. When I was coming up, we only had a bathtub in the main bathroom, and my parents had a tiny shower stall in their bathroom. I always preferred their shower stall to the tub, but hated bumping my elbows into the wall. So, when I started getting big paychecks, I got me a big shower. Check this out."

With a remote sitting on the shelf near the shower stall door, music began to play and lights came on in the shower only. Gina played with the colors until she settled on a soothing blue. She then turned to Michael and told him to take his clothes off.

Once Gina entered the shower stall with Michael, he knew it was on. He relished the feel of the water hitting him from the front and back, but when Gina turned on the rainfall and started kissing him, he knew this session was going to be one for the books. The music, the lights, the warm water, and the sexy woman pressed up against him was overloading all of his senses.

And apparently, the same was happening for Gina. They didn't hear the doorbell, or hear when Janette used her key to enter the house. They didn't hear her call out, or enter the room or the bathroom.

Gina was bracing against the shower bench on one wall. While she had turned the spray jets off, water was still flowing form the rainfall shower head and the music continued to fill the room. Michael had one hand gripping her hip while guiding himself in and out of her, and the other hand gently massaging her clit. Neither of them heard Janette call out Gina's name in the bedroom because of the sounds of Gina's moaning mingled with the music as she reached orgasm. Michael came right after her and gripped her to him until he could barely stand any longer, the two of them in their own world of ecstasy. They were both startled when they heard Janette drop the glass of iced tea she had snagged off of Gina's dresser onto the tile floor, accompanied by her shouts of "Oh my God".

SIXTEEN

There was some chaos and frenzy Janette backed out of the bathroom, left the room and retreated to the living room. Michael carefully stepped out of the shower and threw a towel over the glass on the floor. He handed Gina a towel and then began to scoop up as much of the glass as he could so that she could safely leave the room. Gina dried off in her bedroom, grabbed additional towels for Michael and then got dressed. Her face was pinched with embarrassment.

Janette sat in the living room stunned and silent for several minutes until Gina walked in. "Who knew you could get down like that? Damn!"

"Don't start, Janette!" Gina spat before sitting down.

"That's why I haven't heard for you. You've been getting busy with that dude from JJ's party. From your office. What's his name? Michael."

"Janette, it's not what you think." She saw the look that Janette threw at her. "Ok, it's exactly what you think." She didn't know what to say next.

"Why didn't you tell me about him?" Janette's tone had become serious.

"I didn't tell you because it's not a big deal. I was having a little fun. I was going to tell you when he leaves."

Janette looked closely at her friend. She looked fresh, and definitely had a glow, even after all the commotion. Michael quietly came into the room and stood behind Gina, placing a hand on her shoulder. He nodded to Janette, but spoke directly to Gina.

"I cleaned up as much of the glass as I could. Do a quick vacuum to get any small piece I may have missed. I'm heading out and I'll call you later. Sorry about the drama."

Gina stood and walked him to the door. She thanked him and gave him a quick hug before he left.

Janette sat watching the scene and saying nothing until Gina turned to face her.

"What in the entire hell was that?" Janette asked.

"Why are you here Janette?"

"I came to borrow a platter to take to Eli's for brunch. I couldn't find mine. And, since I've barely talked to you in the past couple of weeks, I figured we could catch up while you got ready. At least I know what's been keeping you so busy."

Gina finally sat down. "Look, I decided to step out of my box. At your suggestion, by the way. And I was going to tell you. Eventually."

"So, what is this? Are you guys a couple?"

"Uh, no! We're just two adults doing adult things. It was our little secret. And I didn't want anyone's opinion about me and a young, sexy man."

"I wouldn't have judged you. Much. And it's one adult one young'un" Janette laughed.

"Whatever," Gina said while rolling her eyes at Janette. "It was consensual sex between adults. No attachments, no drama. Until you showed up."

"Well, I just have one question- was he good? Cause he looked like he knew what the hell he was doing."

Gina sighed, and then slid down in the chair and threw her head back. "Yes, girl, he was good. So very, very good."

Janette tried to keep a straight face before both women erupted in a fit of laughter.

OUT OF OFFICE

1

"I can't believe it was just a month ago when I caught you getting busy in your bathroom with your boy toy. How are things going with you guys?"

"Why not talk a little louder so the people in the back of the plane can hear you better?" Gina said. She turned and scowled at the man in the seat across the aisle as he leaned on his armrest and turned towards the pair, clearly interested in their conversation.

"Oh come one, G, you've been so busy with the launch and saying goodbye to your Hot Boy these last couple of weeks. I know I don't have the full story." Janette was not going to let her friend off he hook.

"You do have the story. I had a 'thing' this summer. It was good. And fun. Gawd, was it fun," Gina sighed, "but now it's over." She turned to the man who was still listening without shame. "It's over."

"I don't know girl, seems like he would've been happy to keep things going." Janette said.

Gina pulled a travel blanket out of the large fancy tote

bag under her seat and wrapped it around herself. She had spent most of the night trying to figure out what to pack for their weeklong stay in Vegas. Janette was giving the keynote address at a women's conference, and she invited her best friend to come along as her Plus One. They hadn't taken a trip together in a while, and they were both ready for some fun and good old fashioned bonding. And since the conference didn't start until Wednesday, they would have two days to check Las Vegas out together and do a little shopping. Or a lot of shopping if Janette had her way.

"Did I thank you for inviting me on this trip?" Gina asked as she reclined her seat. They had been in the air for about twenty minutes, and she was finally able to relax. While she generally didn't mind flying, take off and landing made her super nervous. Now, all she wanted to do was catch up on the sleep she didn't get last night. She wanted to be rested and ready to go once they got settled into their hotel. This was her first trip to Vegas and she didn't want to miss a thing.

"Yes, like twenty times already. I need this as much as you do. I swear, it seems like we've both been operating in overdrive for the last year. That's why I was so shocked that you had a fling with Michael. You've barely had time to breathe, and then I find out you've been humping a hot boy. Literally. I mean, he's what, like thirty years younger than you, right?"

Gina elbowed Janette, while laughing. "Um, he's twenty-three years younger than me."

"So he's about the same age you were when you had JJ? Huh. Interesting."

"Not today, Satan," Gina said as the flight attend
approached to take their drink order.

"Well," Janette said after the flight attendant moved
on, "apparently, you aren't the only with a fetish for
young men. Did I tell you about Jessica Leonard?"

Gina adjusted her blanket, "What about Jessica?"

Jessica Leonard was known for being *the* socialite of
Charleston, and not much else. And since Janette was the
deputy mayor for the city, she was often in the know
regarding the comings and goings of their fine citizens.
"So, I saw her and this young looking guy one night downtown. Bumped into them when I was on Market Street
when my cousin was in town last week. We were at the bar
at Henry's when I saw her in a corner hugged up. I really
couldn't see the guy well, at first. When she headed for the
restroom, I followed her to get the 411. The young man was
cute, and she said she had decided to try 'something new'
to get back out there after her husband left her for his
secretary. She said he wasn't the brightest bulb, but that
she wasn't dating him for his intellect." Janette's laugh was
loud and raunchy, and the guy across the aisle joined in.

Gina shot him a dirty look before she asked, "How
young was he?"

Janette accepted her drink from the flight attendant
and took a sip before she answered. "He was young
enough to still be rocking a fresh Citadel buzz cut." The
Citadel was the military college located in the heart of
Charleston.

Gina gasped, but leaned in for more.

"That young?"

"Girl, he was a couple years past being legal. And

total hotness. Blonde, tanned, and preppy. You can tell from looking at him that the only work that boy does is taking his daddy's boat in and out of the dock."

"Damn. Jessica always liked a pretty boy. They're just usually around her age." Gina clucked.

"Right?" Janette sang. "But really, I don't know about this younger man/older woman thing. What do you do with them besides have sex? What do you talk about?"

"Maybe you should try dating a younger man," Gina said. "I'm not saying rob a cradle, but maybe find a man a few years younger. We're at that age where we can be self-ish. And, it's nobody's business." Gina smiled to herself at she considered the amazing sex she had with Michael.

Janette shrugged, "I don't know. Really never gave it much thought."

"Really, the way you check out men? I'm surprised."

"I appreciate a good looking man, but I'm not always thinking about sleeping with them."

Gina choked a little on the soda she was sipping. "Exactly who do you think you're talking to?" She laughed as she wiped her mouth.

"Ok," Janette smiled, "but a young one? I'on know. I think it'd feel weird. It would be like sleeping with JJ. No offense," she reached out a hand and touched her friend's arm. "I'm not sure I can get my head around someone so young. I'm not knocking your hustle girl."

Gina rolled her eyes at her bestie, "It's not your head you need to get around a younger man, it's your legs. And trust me, all of your preconceived notions will go right out of your head as soon as his dick hits that..."

"Gina!" Janette stage whispered, and then nodded her head towards the man across from them totally engrossed in their conversation. He wasn't even trying to pretend any more.

Gina laughed, "I don't care about him. This is about you. Besides, I'm on vacation. And he don't know me. Seriously though, I know this a work week for you, but if you get the chance to have some fun, I think you should take it. While you've got that 'maintenance' thing on lock with a couple of go to's, I don't hear about you being out here dating and pushing the envelope anymore. It doesn't even sound like you're having fun. And to be honest, you work as much as I do."

Gina pulled the covers up other chin to signal the end of the conversation, while Janette turned and looked out the window. She didn't want to admit that maybe Gina was right. Her routine of work, gym, home, with an occasional tryst with ex lover could definitely be considered a rut. It seemed her job as deputy mayor didn't leave her much time for fun. Sure, she attended a lot of events, and was always out, but it was all work related. She couldn't remember the last time she'd gone out for fun, and it had been eighteen months since she'd taken a proper vacation. She'd talked Gina into coming to the conference with her so that they could have some time together, but it was Gina who thought they should arrive a couple of days early so that they could really hang. Janette looked over at her friend who had somehow actually managed to fall asleep. She tucked the blanket into the corner of the seat for her. At that moment, she decided that maybe her best friend was right. She hadn't had much fun in her dating life lately. Maybe it was time to change that.

2

Gina and Jay wasted no time unpacking once they checked into the hotel. They had a suite with two separate rooms and a common living area.

"Oh my God," Gina said," this place is amazing!" She walked over to the window and looked out on the city. They were on the thirty-fourth floor with an amazing view. Most of the hotels in Charleston had six floors or less. That was the price you pay for living in a city that was below sea level.

"Girl, stop acting like you've never been anywhere before," Janette laughed, as she headed towards her room. They had agreed that they'd get settled in check out the hotel and then have dinner for their first night of girl time.

"I know that I said I would check out the hotel with you, but I think I'm going to take a real nap instead. If you've been in one hotel you've pretty much been in all of them," Janette said.

"Actually, that's not a bad idea. I didn't sleep as well

on the plane as I would have liked because I felt like the creepy guy across from us was watching me the whole time."

"He was. But damn, what have we become? We're acting like two old ladies."

Gina laughed," Guess you're right. How about this, we take a nap and then we hit up a bar after dinner for drinks and dancing?"

"Now you're talking. And I don't want to hear any excuses from you later about how you're so tired because we are going out- out."

"Deal. See you at 7:30," Gina said before she closed the door to her room.

By the time Janette came out of her room a couple of hours later, she was starving but well rested. She hoped that Gina wasn't going to take all night, but much to her surprise, Gina opened her door at exactly 7:30 looking fresh and ready to go.

"Well, I guess sleep does a body good," Janette said. "That and recent good sex."

Gina ignored Janette's comments and twirled. She was wearing a black tank top with spaghetti straps, matching black wide palazzo pants, and silver scrappy sandals. She had a black silk wrap in one hand and a small silver evening bag in the other. Her hair was piled on top of her head and her kinky curls were shiny and defined. She really did look gorgeous.

"Well, you don't look so bad yourself. If I had your legs, girl, I'd be halfway dangerous!" Gina laughed. Janette was barely five feet, two inches, but she had great legs, and she loved to show them off in short dresses and skirts. Her short hair was was perfectly styled, and she was currently wearing a yellow high-low halter dress with wedges. Her toned arms screamed "I work out". She grabbed her pink crossbody bag and slung it over her shoulder.

"Wait, are you really taking that to dinner?" Gina asked.

"What?"

"That bag?"

"Yep, especially since we're going dancing afterwards. Hands-free and I know where my stuff is at all times."

Gina looked thoughtful and said, "Give me a minute." She walked into her room and was back in less than a minute. She'd changed into a pair of silver wedges and had items in her hand. She walked over to Janette, gave her credit card, a wad of money, her room card, and her driver's license.

"Here, put these in your purse. And let's go, we're going to be late, and we don't want to lose our reservations."

"And why can't you carry your own shit?" Janette asked.

"I don't have a crossbody that would match this outfit."

She was across the room and out the door before Janette could finish saying "You get on my damn nerves."

Janette felt like she was stuffed from dinner and thought that maybe she could talk Gina out of going dancing. It was just Monday night, and they'd have tomorrow night before the conference started. She would have been content with an evening stroll, or finally checking out the hotel. But Gina wasn't having it, and had asked the waiter for a nearby club recommendation before they finished paying their bill.

"We're in Las Vegas, so we're going to do Vegas stuff. Besides, it's only 10:00. I'm not sleepy after that long nap. I'm horrible at gambling, and I can watch Netflix at home."

They waited in line at the club for over twenty minutes before they finally reached the man at the door. He gave them a once over and raised his eyebrows, but Gina then stood on her tiptoes and whispered something into the man's ear and slipped him some money. He smiled and stepped aside, slipping the money Gina gave him in his pocket. Before Janette could ask what that was all about, she took in the decor. It looked like every club in Charleston could fit in this one space. The club was swanky and slick, and the beat hit them at the door. Janette looked around and shook her head. The place was packed and everyone appeared to be in motion.

"I'm not sure about this," she yelled to Gina.

"We're doing this!" Gina yelled back and then began to make her way to the nearest bar. Janette followed, wondering when her friend had become so damn bold. By the time she caught up to Gina at the bar, she heard her tell the bar tender "two".

"What are you ordering?" Janette asked.

"Tequila shots."

"Tequila?! You know I don't mess with tequila. That is so not a good look for me."

"And that's exactly why we're starting with it. And don't switch to anything else because I am not putting a cold cloth on your neck while you puke all night long. Tequila only. We start with shots and then you can switch to cocktails. With tequila."

Janette shook her head. There seemed to be no reasoning with Gina tonight. She'd been joking for a month that sleeping with a younger man had rocked Gina's world, but she realized that she had not seen this side of Gina since college. She briefly thought about what she would have done back in the day as the bartender returned with two shots. She looked and Gina, who had a goofy smile on her face, but clearly seemed to be enjoying herself, picked up the glass, and then toasted her friend before taking the shot.

She shook herself from the initial burn and then caught the bartender's attention and asked for two more.

Gina whooped, and did a shimmy. Janette laughed, and then said, "When in Rome."

Minutes after the second shot, Janette felt herself warming up and getting loose. The music was infectious and she was ready to dance. Gina had been surveying the men on the floor, and had even rejected a couple who had asked her to dance.

"You can't stand here all night," she said to Janette. "You need to get out there."

"Yeah, let's go," Janette said, grabbing Gina's hand.

Gina shook her head. "Not with me, girl. Some guy. Find someone you're interested in and ask him to dance." She was talking in Janette's ear so that she could hear her.

"This is our trip, I'm not looking for a guy. Come Gee, let's dance."

Gina smiled. "I dare you to find a young looking guy and ask him to dance."

"What?" Janette was sure her friend was up to something.

"I said, I dare you to ask a young guy to dance. Every guy here should be at least 21 to be here, so, do it. I dare you. You've been riding me all month long about getting busted with Michael. But when was the last time you stepped out of your box? We're in Vegas. You are out of the office for a whole week. I won't tell if you won't." Gina's grin looked damn near diabolical. But she also knew that Janette seldom backed down from a dare.

"Dance with a dude? No problem. I got that."

"And make out with him."

"What? Girl no! I'm not doing that."

"I dare you. In fact, I'll pay for our next vacation- all expenses, your pick, if you do it."

Janette looked at Gina as if she had horns coming out of her head. "What is wrong with you? You're going to let me choose our next vacation spot if I kiss a random guy? You can't be serious."

"I am. Anyplace. On me. But he has to be younger than us." Gina ordered a third round of shots while she waited for Janette to answer.

Janette shook her head, but then thought about it. Gina was offering up a free trip? How silly! But the more she thought about it, the more the question 'why not' kept coming up.

"Ok Gina, it's a deal. I'll do it. But I pick the guy. Not you."

Gina shrugged, and then extended her hand for a shake to officially seal the deal. She then handed Janette a third shot.

It took Janette a few minutes of scanning the room before she found a potential target. It seemed that at some point, he began watching her watch him. He was an average height, pecan tan, and a close beard. She wondered when beards became so popular. If she had to guess his age, she'd say he was about twenty-five. He had on a white short-sleeved button down shirt, slim fitting distressed jeans, and a pair of suede chukka boots. His fro was somewhat high with closely shaved sides that were edged to precision. He looked like he had just stepped out of the pages of a mens magazine. She continued to scan the room, but her eyes kept coming back to him.

"Quit looking and decide," Gina nudged her, as a tall black man with an all gray fade settled next to Gina. He said hello to them both and then asked Gina if he could buy her and her friend a drink.

"My friend's about to dance, but sure, I'll take a drink." Gina gave Janette a small shove in the direction of the dance floor. Janette looked back and Gina finger waved to her. She then turned to the guy at the bar and leaned in to start chatting him up. She seemed relaxed and confident. Janette wasn't sure if it was the tequila or a new and improved Gina.

Janette squared her shoulders and figured that the best thing to do would be to just get on with it, as she walked over to the man in the white shirt. Instead of speaking, she grabbed his hand and pulled him to his feet. One of his friend's looked at her and yelled, "so it's like that?" She shrugged one shoulder and hoped the white shirt guy would still follow her. He did.

The DJ was playing a heavy hip-hop mix, and while Janette didn't love the words, the bass and the tequila gave her plenty to work with. Within a few minutes, she was feeling her own self with her shimmy and hip moves, throwing in a few bounces. When a new DJ started playing salsa music, she figured the guy wouldn't be able to hang and was about to call it quits, but he grabbed her hand and began to lead her around the floor. As they twirled across the floor, she was aware of the heat from his hand along the small of her back. He had sexy moves, and he led her well. He watched her intently, never daring to converse over the music and the movement. By the time the DJ had changed things up again, she realized that she had been on the floor for over an hour.

She reached up to hug the young man, and as she wrapped her arms around his neck, she remembered the other part of the bet. She was still high from the dancing and drinking and figured *what the hell*, so she turned her head and kissed him on the lips. The young man pulled back surprised, but then leaned in and kissed her full and proper, with his tongue slipping in her mouth. She responded in kind, and then felt a full warmth spread through her body as he gently sucked on her tongue. For a minute, she forgot that she was in the middle of a club with a stranger.

She finally pulled away and walked back to the bar, where she ordered another drink, and scanned the floor for her friend. She hoped that Gina had seen the whole thing,

4

Janette had eventually found Gina on the dance floor with the Silver Fox, as Gina called him later that night, and managed to convince her it was time to go. They called for a ride back to their hotel and spent the time in the car laughing about the events of the night. Both women were still a bit tipsy by the time they got up to their suite and crashed.

When Janette got up the following morning, there was a note from Gina saying she'd gone down to breakfast and reserved a cabana for them at the pool. Janette took her time getting dressed. She had consumed more tequila last night than she had in the entire year. She felt dehydrated and headachy, and cracked open a bottle of water before slipping on her swimsuit and going down to the pool.

She found Gina posted up in the shade, wearing an African print tankini and large sunglasses. Her hair was down, but she was wearing a scrunci on her wrist, just in case.

"Look who decided to finally roll out of bed," Gina said as Janette approached. "It's almost lunch time. I thought I was going to have to come up and get you. How you feeling'?"

Janette took off her wrap and eased her body onto the lounger. "Like I worked out with Mike Tyson. My hips and ass are sore. I haven't shaken it like that in a long time."

"Girl, you were killing it out there. But that young thang sure did keep up with you."

"I handled my business, didn't I?" Janette laughed. She opened the bottle of water she brought with her and took a sip.

"You did. And I saw that kiss, too." Gina smirked as she turned her body towards Janette. "That was hot. I thought that boy was going to take you right there on the dance floor."

Janette smiled. "I can't believe I did that. You're a bad influence girl."

"I'm a bad influence? A couple of months ago you were telling me I needed to get under a young thing, and now you're acting all school girlish about kissing one? Girl, please."

"Oh come on, Gina, I don't think I ever really thought you'd have sex with Michael. I was just joking. But I ain't gonna lie, it's like a switch has been flipped for you. You're acting brand new on me."

"I'm not acting brand new, I'm acting like I'm not dead. Michael reminded me that I've still got a lot of gas to burn. I'm having fun. My son is traipsing around the world doing good, I have a business that's flourishing, and the privilege of time and money. This is what we've been working so hard towards. I'm finally seeing that. We work hard, so we need to play even harder."

Janette looked out at the pool while she nibbled on some of the food that Gina had ordered and watched people frolicking in the water. Gina's words were hitting her right between the eyes. She didn't have children or a husband, by choice. She had never regretted those decisions because it allowed her to do all the things she wanted without guilt or worry about the needs of others, but lately she'd only been focused on work. She was surprised at how she'd left work take over her life.

"Well, last night I kissed a random guy at a club after dancing for over an hour, so I'd say that I'm playing hard right now. And I'm going to take a great trip in the future because of it."

Gina sat up and nudged her friend on the arm. "Looks like your dance floor buddy is coming this way."

"What?" Janette said in surprise. She turned over and looked in the direction of the hotel doors she came out of. Sure enough, the guy she had been dancing with the night before was walking in their direction. He was wearing swim trunks and had a towel in one hand and a room key card and phone in the other.

"Don't draw attention to him. He probably doesn't even remember what I look like," Janette said as he neared their loungers.

"Well, good morning young man, didn't my friend and I see you last night?" Gina called out, causing Janette to freeze.

The man stopped and looked to his left. He glanced at Gina and then Janette, and then he smiled. "Hi," he said, coming over to stand at the foot of their chairs.

Gina extended her hand, "I'm Gina, and this is my best friend, Janette." He reached down and shook her hand and then looked over at Janette.

Janette sat up fully and placed her feet on the concrete. She stood up and shook his hand. She needed to take control of this situation before Gina had her in another stupid situation.

"I'm Janette," she said. "Thanks for the dancing last night."

"I'm Grayson." He continued to smile as he looked at her. "You have some moves. I had to break out my A Game last night."

"And what a game it was," Gina said softly. Janette shot her a warning look. Gina took the hint and got up. "Excuse me for a moment, I seem to have forgotten my book. I'll be back shortly." She grabbed her keycard, slipped on her flip flops and headed into the hotel. Janette grimaced to herself. She couldn't be any more obvious.

"You here for business or pleasure," Grayson asked after Gina left. He sat across from Janette, on Gina's newly vacated lounger. Janette hesitated, then sat back down.

"Here for a conference. How about yourself." What was she doing? It wasn't like this conversation was going to lead to anything. Why was she bothering?

"Nah. I'm here on vacay with my boys. I'm starting a new gig soon, and one of my friends is getting married next month, so it's kind of a bachelor party/celebration thing."

"I see." Janette didn't know what else to say. "Well it was great meeting you, Grayson. I hope you enjoy the rest of your vacation." Janette hoped that he would take the hint. Last night was over and she'd had a good time.

"Yeah," he said, "uh, have a good time at your conference." He stood and looked down at her for a moment. "Um, Janette, how about we hang out tonight?"

Her brow furrowed. "Hang out? You and me? Tonight?"

Grayson smiled. "Yes, Janette. I'd like to see you again. And it's obvious that we're staying in the same hotel." He held up the towel and keycard. "So, I figure since we're both gonna be here for a few days, we can hang out. You seem fun. And I like having fun." The bass in his voice had dropped considerably.

Janette bit the inside of her lip. He couldn't possibly be thinking what she thought he was thinking. "So, thanks for the offer Grayson, but I'm gonna have to say no."

"Why?"

"Why what?"

"Why do you have to say no? Are you married? I didn't see a ring last night. Don't see one now."

Ok, Janette thought, so this dude is cocky. "Nope. I'm not married. And last night, well, last night my girlfriend dared me to ask you to dance," she figured it would be best to leave the part about the kissing out, "and I did. We danced and had a good time. That's it."

"Uh huh," he said, "so you're a woman who knows what she wants. I like that. And don't forget that kiss, by the way. It was perfection."

Janette shook her head. What in the entire hell was happening?

"How about this," Grayson continued, "you let me

show you a good time since you made my night last night? And none of my friends have bet me to ask you out." He looked totally serious.

"Really Grayson, I'm sure you and your friends have plenty to get into this week."

He nodded, "We do, but tonight I want to hang out with a beautiful woman, not my friends. They'll be fine."

Janette searched Grayson's face for the lie. He stood patiently, as if he knew that she would eventually give in.

"How old are you, Grayson?" She had to ask.

"Twenty-five, why?"

Janette had definitely called it when she saw him last night.

"Because I'm fifty-two." She figured that she didn't need to say more.

"Great, so you're legal. Got it. Glad we got that out of the way. What's your room number? I'll pick you up around 9:00."

Janette had to laugh at the audacity. After a few thoughtful moments, she responded, "Ok, Grayson, I'll play. But for the record, let's just keep it light. I don't need to know the details of your life, and you don't need to know mine. We have fun tonight, and that's it. I'll meet you in the lobby at 9."

Grayson flashed his pearly whites at her again, and she had to admit that he was indeed charming. "Keep it light. Keep it fun. Got it. So how about you let me take it from here, and um, wear something casual and comfy." He stood up and grabbed his things and headed for the other side of the pool to a set of chairs directly across from her.

When Janette exited the elevators at exactly 8:59pm, she saw Grayson sitting in an easy chair facing the elevator doors. His eyes roamed appreciatively over her simple outfit of skinny jeans, a silk tank top, and wedges. Her short hair was messy in an intentional way. She oozed confidence and sexiness. He stroked his beard as he stood to greet her.

"You look hot," he said, and leaned down to give her a hug.

Janette laughed, "Thanks, I did as instructed. Casual and comfy."

"Have you had dinner yet?"

"Yeah, I had an early dinner with Gina, so I'm not really hungry. But I could always eat dessert."

He nodded, "Well, how about we work up an appetite, and then we can get you that dessert. Or a nightcap. Or both." He placed his hand on the small of her back and guided her towards the lobby doors.

Grayson's take charge attitude was definitely appealing.

They snagged a cab that was idling outside of the hotel and Grayson told the driver to take them to the MGM Grand hotel.

"So we're leaving one hotel for another?" Janette asked as they got on their way.

"You'll see," he said.

They talked about how they each spent the rest of their day on the short drive, and then Grayson asked what she did for a living.

"Uh uh, no personal stuff, remember," Janette said.

"Right. Because you don't want me stalking you when you go back home."

Janette took her time before she spoke, "Because this is Vegas and we're having fun. That's all." She grabbed his hand to emphasize her point.

"Then I guess I better do this while I've got the chance." He stroked her hand with his other hand and then leaned in to kiss her. The kiss was slow and tender and he wrapped his arms around her and pulled her close.

Instead of pulling back, Janette found herself snaking her arms around his neck. She found herself melting into him. Her nipples hardened and her clit began to throb. She was definitely feeling hot for him. They continued kissing until the cab stopped in front of the hotel. Grayson paid the driver, and then helped her out of the cab. They walked into the hotel and took a left, and headed into a bar called Level 21.

There were signs outside the entrance informing

patrons that they had to be twenty-one to enter, but inside was an arcade and bar atmosphere. There were game tables all around, gaming machines at the bar, pool and ping pong tables, virtual reality games and even karaoke. Janette gave Grayson a confused look.

"What are we doing here?"

"We're going to play games. And have fun. Come on." He pulled her towards an air hockey table and settled her in. I'll be right back with a drink. What'll you have?"

"I'll have a margarita," Janette figured sticking with tequila wouldn't be a bad thing on this trip. It had served her well last night.

Grayson came back with her drink and a beer for himself. He also had tokens for the games. He took a couple of swigs from his beer before he started talking trash.

"Finish your drink, Janette, and then let me see what you got. And I hope you lose well."

"Lose? Oh yeah, you've just met me. You have no idea what I'm capable of." Janette set her drink down and grabbed the paddle. When Grayson was ready, she hit the puck and started the game. She beat him three games out of five, before he decided that they needed to move on to something else.

They played Ms. Pac-Man, Space Invaders, beer pong, and even sang karaoke. Janette could not remember the last time she had so much fun. When they got back to the hotel, they hit up the dessert bar and even had a few more drinks. They were both more than a little tipsy when they realized that it was after 1am.

"I really need to go up to my room. My conference

starts tomorrow. I'm gonna look like a hot mess if I don't get some sleep.

Grayson reached out to touch her face, "I doubt you could ever look like a hot mess." He leaned over and kissed her, one hand on her thigh and the other on the back of her neck. "How about we go up to my room?" He kissed her again before she could answer.

Her head was already fuzzy from the alcohol and sugar, but her body was reacting to his touch. And she liked it and wanted more of it.

"I'm not sure that's a good idea," she said between kisses.

"Room 2449. Grayson Williams. Text it to your friend. Tell her where you are and who you're with." Grayson pulled away from her to let her know that he was serious.

Janette looked at him and considered his words. She had to admit that she was extremely attracted to him, and it was obvious that he was attracted to her. The idea of being with Grayson was more than exciting.

"We need ground rules before we do this," she said.

He kissed her again. "You like rules. I like you. So we'll play by your rules. I just hope you don't have too many. I don't want to waste this." He discreetly grabbed her hand and placed it between his legs. She felt his erection and became even more excited. So much so that she then slid her hand down to cup his balls.

"No kinky sex. No unprotected sex. And if I say stop, we stop. No questions asked."

He briefly closed his eyes as she gave his balls a gentle squeeze. "That leaves a whole lot that we can do. Let's go." He grabbed the hand on his balls and pulled her to the elevator.

He pressed the call button and then pulled her in front of him. "Text your friend now. I'm not kidding. I don't want anything to stop you from letting me have my way with you." He began kissing her on her neck as she pulled out her phone and clumsily texted Gina.

They began taking off their clothes as soon as they entered his room. He wasn't in a fancy suite, but his room was still large with a view of the city lights. He was going to close the curtains when Janette instructed him to leave them open. She shimmied out of her jeans, kicked them off, and pulled her tank over her head while she watched him step out of his own jeans. He was wearing boxer briefs and was about to pull them down when she stopped him.

"Let me," she said, and then walked over and slowly pulled his underwear down. His large dick bounced free as he helped her finish taking them off. He watched her, in anticipation of what would come next. She unsnapped her bra and took off her panties, and then reached out to stroke his hard dick. He swayed a little at her touch, and tried to touch her breast.

"Not yet. Grab a condom and lie down." Her voice was husky and her eyes were hooded.

He walked to his suitcase and rooted around until he found a box of condoms. He opened the box and threw a strip on the bed before following her instructions.

Janette slowly walked over to the bed. She knew that her silhouette looked good and curvy against the city lights. When she reached the bed, she opened a condom packet and rolled the condom down Grayson's shaft. He reached out to kiss her, but she pulled back until she was done. Then she climbed on top of him and took her time sliding herself down on his dick. She sighed as he filled her up and then leaned down to kiss him.

She rode him slowly, enjoying the feel of him as he enjoyed her. His control surprised her and increased her excitement. She picked up the pace, riding him and feeling him throb inside of her. When he stroked her with his thumb, she became super wet. When he smiled at her, she could no longer hold back. She leaned down again and started sucking on his nipple. If she couldn't hold it, neither would he.

He gently pinched her clit and her body caught fire. She rocked into him faster and faster and then gently bit him on the nipple. He cried out in pleasure, and it finished her off. Her vagina began to contract around him as her clit pulsed. She bucked and groaned while he moaned quietly and held her hips tightly to him.

When they were done, she rolled off him, kissed him long and slow, and then scooted under the covers. He eventually broke away and went into the bathroom to get rid of the condom. When he returned, he turned her towards him, letting the covers remain between them, and kissed her again. They continued kissing in the entangled sheet until he became hard again.

"Would you like to go again?" he asked.

"If you think you can handle it," she replied with a smile.

Janette eased the door of the suite open. Her plan was to tiptoe to her room and get ready for breakfast and the conference kick off before Gina even stirred. Except Gina was sitting on the sofa in a kimono sipping on a cup of coffee. She was fresh faced and had a glow.

"Oh, I see you decided to finally come home." Gina sipped from her cup and tried to hide her smile. "Care to share what you've been up to all night. Or can I guess? Young man, strong back, presumably a big dick?" She couldn't help but laugh at her own joke.

"Whatever, Gina. I can do what I want." Janette dropped her shoes by the door and walked over and plopped down on the sofa. To her surprise, there was a cup of coffee sitting on the table. The first sip was delicious.

"Hurry up with your caffeination. I need to hear the details before you have to get ready and get out of here. I've already ordered room service, and it should be here shortly. You can talk while we eat."

Janette shook her head. Of course Gina had every-thing under control. She always did. She curled her feet under her and sat back with her cup. "Where would you like me to start?"

"The sex, Hunny, get to the sex. I don't care about your date." Gina laughed.

"Oh my God! Girl. I started off thinking that I was showing him a thing or two, and he was polite enough to let me think that, but guurrrlllll! He showed me some stuff last night. Ohh!" Janette shuddered at the memory of rounds two and three with Grayson.

"I'm listening," Gina said, "and don't leave anything out."

"Ok, well, we went to this arcade bar and played games, sang karaoke, and even played hopscotch. We had a blast. I'm really glad I listened to him and wore comfortable clothes. It was just so much fun. I got to let my hair down."

"And be a kid again, with a kid. I like it."

Janette tossed a throw pillow at Gina. "Shut up, girl. You can't say nothing to me."

"You right, but that doesn't mean I don't have jokes. Continue."

"We were hot and heavy in the bar downstairs. First dessert, then a couple of drinks' and then kissing. But when he reached out and put my hand on his hard ass penis, it was over for me. It felt like a rock, and once I cupped and massaged those balls, I had him." Janette grinned.

"So, you were getting nasty in the bar downstairs? Like you don't have home training?"

"Exactly like that! And as soon as we got to his room I rode him like the stallion he is. Gurl!" Janette giggled

"Well alright now. And then?"

"And then, he fucked me with a slow stroke that almost made me lose my mind!"

"Say what now? Slow stroke?"

"Yes. Good old fashioned 'I'm gonna make you weak in the knees' fucking but not banging. Like you would do to old R&B back in the day."

"Oh my," was the only response Gina could manage.

"Did you and Michael do that?" Janette asked.

"Uh, no. We had good old hot sweaty sex. I was not interested in anything slow and sexy. I wanted the heat." Gina laughed. "I can get slow stroking' somewhere else." A sly smile crossed her face.

"Well, I slept for an hour after round two, but before I left, he ate me out like I was the buffet and he was starving. Seriously, his tongue work was crazy. I can't even remember the last time a guy went down on me without expecting reciprocation. I'm not quite sure how I was able to actually walk out of his room and to the elevator. I have been thoroughly handled. And I liked it." Her smile was huge.

"It's all over your face. But child, you don't need to be doing the Walk of Shame, you need to be doing the Walk of the Shameless. Properly sated and proud of it." Gina cackled again.

"Yeah, but what am I doing, Gee? He's twenty-five." Reality was starting to kick in.

"What are you feeling?"

Janette sort of shrugged, "Part of me feels like it's wrong, and part of me just doesn't care."

"Why is it wrong? He's way past legal. If you were a man, you'd be giving yourself a high five for scoring a hottie, and telling yourself you still got it."

"Damn girl," Janette said, getting up to answer the door after a knock and a room service announcement.

She grabbed her wallet out of her purse, opened the door and signed the slip, and gave the young woman a generous tip. She then carried the tray to the sofa and set it down on the table then she and Gina went in on the food.

"I know you're right. I'm not uncomfortable with him at all. But I did wonder several times last night what other people were thinking."

"It's not other people's business," Gina said between bites of food. "Have fun. Don't think too much about it. Like when we were in our twenties. We didn't lament every time we banged a new guy. Well, you didn't. I was loving James hard, so that was that for me. Where is that girl?"

"She's now in her fifties. With a good job, a mortgage, and a 401k."

"But she's not dead. Your vagina, your rules." Gina raised her coffee cup for a toast, and Janette returned the gesture.

"Enough about me, I feel like I've kind of abandoned you this trip. We were supposed to spend bestie time together. What've you been getting up to? I feel like I should be keeping tabs on you since that whole secret lover thing with Michael."

Gina smiled, "I mean, I'm good. You know I don't have any problems being with myself. But, um, no worries, I've got something to keep me busy while you're off getting smashed."

Janette looked it her watch, "You've got ten minutes before I need to get a shower and get dressed. Spill."

"Ok, well, you know that Silver Fox that I met at the bar our first night while you were lip-locking on the Jr. Model? Well, we had dinner last night. And drinks. And then we just chilled.

"Silver Fox?" Janette frowned trying to remember the guy that Gina was talking about. "You mean the tall dude with the gray hair?"

"That one."

Janette's eyebrows went up, "Ok, ma'am. And."

Gina smiled and leaned back into the sofa, "And I like him. We're getting to know each other. He's retired from the military and works in the business office of his son's construction company in North Carolina. He's here with some old military friends. We click."

"You sure he doesn't have a wife back home? He's attractive and retired."

"His wife passed away about five years ago. His kids wish he'd start dating. They say he spends too much time alone."

"Huh, sounds like two peas in a pod."

"Excuse me?" Gina tried to feign indignant.

"Whatever. You know I'm telling the truth. I'm glad you've found someone to play with because I'm going into conference mode. I'm assuming you have plans today?"

"Yeah, Silver Fox and I are going to see the Hoover Dam, so you aren't the only one who needs to get moving and get ready. We'll probably have dinner together tonight. Unless you want to do something."

"No," Janette said getting up from the sofa, "I think I probably need to spend a night in the room getting some rest. I have to finish polishing up my keynote. I'm not trying to get up there and sound crazy because I haven't made time to put my best foot forward."

"You're gonna kill it, like you always do. But yeah, you might want to spend some time doing some work, since you are, you know, *working*."

Janette's phone buzzed as she picked up her stuff and headed to her room.

"Wow, I guess that dude's calling to get some milk to go with all that cookie you gave him last night and this morning.

"Shut it, Gina," Janette called as she closed the door to her room.

By noon, Janette was feeling the effects of her activities from the night before. While she was enjoying meeting new people and catching up with old friends she really was looking forward to a night in. She was having way more fun than she imagined she would at a conference, thanks to Grayson. Thoughts of him and how he handled her body crept in when she should have been focused on the various break out sessions she was attending. Her trip was no where near over, but she knew that when she returned to Charleston she would feel like Vegas owed her nothing.

As the last session let out, Janette got trapped by a young woman who wanted to speak with her about working in city government. They sat and talked until the hotel staff came in to clean up from the day's activities and set up for the morning sessions. After finally breaking free, Janette made her way to the elevators. Grayson was leaning against a pillar across the from the elevators with his hands in his pockets and a patient look on his face.

"Are you stalking me? Should I call security?" Janette said, her voice getting husky just from his presence.

"I am stalking you. You been running through my mind all day. I kinda like it. Like you liked what I did to you this morning." He licked his lips and then roamed his eyes over her. It was so sexy that Janette found herself wanting to lean over and kiss him.

"So, what're you up to tonight?" Janette needed to change the subject. She was starting to get wet just being near him.

"Official bachelor party stuff. Matter of fact, we're leaving in about thirty minutes. I decided to wait down here, hoping to see you."

"You must have been waiting for a while. I ended up talking with someone after the session."

"I'd wait as long as it would take so see you." He licked his lips again. She really needed to ask him to stop doing that. "Are you and you're bestie hanging out?"

"No, not tonight. I've got to work on my speech, and she's, well, she's suddenly developed plans."

"I see. Well, how about I escort you to your room. You know, just to make sure you get there safe. And of course, give you something to think about while you work." He had a glint in his eye as he walked over to press the elevator button. He turned around and held his hand out to her.

She grabbed it without thinking, just as the doors behind him opened. He pulled her inside and pulled her to him.

"What floor," he said as he reached out one hand towards the floor numbers."

"Thirty-six," Janette said, not bothering to pull away.

Grayson leaned down and kissed her, sliding his hands down her back and then gripping her ass. She felt warm and gooey and dropped her bags on the floor. As he explored her mouth with his tongue, he began to slide her dress up. When he reached her panties, he stuck his hands inside and squeezed her ass like it was PlayDoh. He palmed her pussy, and she gasped when his finger found its way to her clit, and then smoothly entered her. He never broke the kiss, and as he fingered her and tiny moans escaped from her. She held onto his neck and relished the feel of his fingers and his lips until the elevator stopped on her floor. She was happy that it had not stopped for anyone else on the way up.When the doors opened, she stepped back and grabbed her bags and then stood to block the doors from closing.

"Let me walk you to your room," Grayson said. His dimples deepened.

Janette shook her head, "No. We both know that's not a good idea. I won't get any work done, and you would miss the bachelor party."

"How about I text you when I get back?" That grin was challenging her resistance.

"No."

"Ok, well how about dinner tomorrow night? It's my last night in town. I'm leaving late Friday morning."

Janette looked thoughtful, "What about your friends?"

"They would all ditch me to spend time with a beautiful woman. They'll be fine." He stepped to her and kissed her again.

"Ok, ok. I've got to go do some work. We'll do dinner tomorrow."

"Good. One last thing,"

"No, Grayson," Janette laughed.

"Give me something to tide me over until tomorrow night."

"Like?"

He leaned down and whispered in her ear while sliding his hand back up her dress, "Like these silky panties." He then started to slide them down as he kissed her again. He held the door open with one hand as he waited for her to step out of them. Janette could not believe the she was even doing it.

"You are so nasty," she said, handing over a pair of her favorite panties. He stuffed them in his back pocket while she grabbed her purse and bag and stepped out into the hall.

"And you like it," he said as the doors closed on his handsome grinning face.

"I can't believe you gave that boy your panties," Gina laughed as she watched Janette getting dressed.

"And I can't believe you spent all day sending swimsuit pics to the Silver Fox. What are y'all doing tonight anyway?"

Gina shrugged, "Don't much know. I'm thinking some drinks at the bar. Maybe more dancing.

"Well, I didn't realize how good looking that man truly was until last night."

Gina and her new friend had decided to spend time in the suite last night. Janette had finished her keynote speech and was flipping through the tv channels when Gina arrived with her friend. They talked with Janette for a few minutes before pouring a couple of glasses of wine and going out onto the balcony. When Janette gathered her things to head to her room, she heard her friend's laughter and saw her ease with her guest. She was happy for Gina.

"Is he planning to give your panties back at dinner?"

Gina asked, bring the conversation back to Janette and Grayson. "Cause that really would be nasty."

"No crazy lady, he can keep the panties. Matter of fact, forget about the panties."

"Ok. So are you gonna fuck him again?"

"Real mature, Gina. But um, hell yeah!" Janette laughed. "It's been a really good trip. May as well go out with a bang."

"Or in your case, with getting banged. And then?"

"Then nothing. What happened next with you and Michael? He's in Austin living his life, and you're in Charleston living yours. Everybody's happy. It was what it was."

"Except, I think you kind of like him, like him."

"What do you mean? I like him enough to sleep with him, sure."

"Nope, I think this guy has your nose open. You're smiling for no reason, all giddy, like you're high school crushing. Michael was good for me because he reminded me that I'm still a vibrant woman. You already knew that. So what else is this guy doing for you besides making Miss Kitty tighten up?"

Janette sat on the bed for a moment. She wasn't sure she was ready to be honest with herself, let alone with Gina. She decided to dive in, because Gina would know if she was lying anyway. "Girl, I hate to say it, but this guy is smooth. And romantic. And I feel like he's totally *with me* when we're together. Like he's genuinely interested in me and wants me to know how much. It's been a while since I had that. Since I even wanted that."

Gina nodded, "I mean, but it's not like you've been in a drought."

"No, I haven't been in a sex drought, but these last few days I have realized that I've been in a romance drought. I mean, when was the last time you had a man waiting around just to spend a few minutes with you in his busy day? Telling you how beautiful he thinks you are. Making time for you instead of fitting you in. I know it's been a long ass time for me."

"Damn. Same."

"I've been getting maintenance, but I haven't been interested in a real relationship with the couple of guys on my roster. And don't get me wrong, I'm not thinking relationship possibilities with this guy, but I am realizing that it's not off the table for me with the right guy."

"Well, alright now!" Gina said and gave her friend a high-five. "Shut up and put your face on and get ready to give this young thing the night of his life. Give him something to tell his friends about."

"The way things have been going, he's going to give me something to tell *you* about."

"And I will be here ready to drink all the tea!" Gina laughed.

Grayson grabbed her hand as they walked back to the hotel from the restaurant. She was wearing a black one shoulder dress and strappy heels. She felt and looked super feminine. Instead of pearls, she'd opted for a dainty gold necklace, and large gold hoop earrings. He couldn't seem to stop staring at her.

"I know you said no real life info this week, but how about next week when we're back to our real lives? I'd at least like to be able to say 'hi' on occasion." He gently swung their hands back and forth as they walked.

Janette turned her head to the side and smiled. She was glad that he wanted to stay in touch. "I mean, I guess we can text or talk every now and then."

"Every now and then, huh?

"I mean, what, you're not trying to call me every day, are you?"

"And what if I was? Would you have a problem with that?"

Janette looked over at him, "I guess I wouldn't," she said softly.

They continued to walk in silence, holding hands and taking in the sights until they arrived back at the hotel. In the elevator, he just held her close and pressed the number 24 for his floor.

"Grayson, I can't spend the night with you. I have to be fresh for my keynote tomorrow."

"I know. I just want to give you a proper goodbye is all. I promise, it won't take all night. Unless you change your mind."

She stayed pressed against his chest, feeling his strong arms wrapped around her body. She wanted nothing more than to stay all night. "Just for a little while, then."

There was a silver tray with a single red rose, and two wine glasses sitting on the dresser. Next to it was a bottle of wine and a plate of chocolate covered strawberries. There was a faint glow of light from the lamp on the bedside table.

"What's this?" Janette asked, with a smile.

"Just in case you were interested in a drink. But really, I wanted to spend a few minutes of quiet time with you. I wanted to let you know how much I've enjoyed you these past few days. I'm interested in getting to know you. And, I'm hoping that once you get home, you'll realize that you want the same thing as well."

Janette didn't say anything as she slid open the glass doors and stepped onto the small balcony. There were concrete walls on either side to protect the occupants' privacy, and two rattan chairs with cushions in each corner. Janette turned to face Grayson, wrapping her arms around him and kissing him.

"Thank you for a great time this week," she murmured into his neck. His cologne was light and intoxicating.

"Thank you for asking me to dance. You started this whole thing."

"I didn't ask you to dance. I pulled you on the dance floor. But you're welcome."

"So you like being right, huh?" He asked, gently moving her hair across her forehead.

"I do. Just like you like making me hot."

"Yeah, I do like that." He kissed her cheek, her neck, and then gently bit her on the ear. She shuddered involuntarily, and then took his lower lip between her teeth. She gently bit it, and then kissed him. She broke the kiss and turned around and pulled his arms around her. They stood that way, looking at the lights, until she felt his dick harden against her ass. She pushed against him and turned around and started to unbuckle and unzip his pants. She pulled out his penis and stroked it. It jumped in her hand. She wanted to feel him inside of her one last time. She pushed him back towards one of the chairs without a word. She took her shoes off and kneeled in front of him on the cushion from the other chair, wrapped her hand around his shaft, and took him in her mouth. She bobbed her head as she sucked his dick, swirling her tongue around the head, while he gripped the edges of the chair.

"Baby, stop, or you're gonna make me cum," he said, with a deep growl.

"Oh, you are definitely going to cum," she said when she pulled back she stood. She had pulled a condom from her dress pocket, ripped it open, and rolled it down his pulsing dick. She then turned around and flipped up her dress and eased herself down. She rocked back and forth, with his cock hitting her g-spot, while he gripped her with both arms. He could feel that she was about to let loose, so he pulled her head against his chest and kissed the spot between her neck and shoulder. His hand snaked down between her legs, lightly flicking her bud. It was exactly what sent her over the edge. He then pumped her hips into him as she came and his release joined hers.

Janette finished her speech to a standing ovation, and she took her seat on the stage, ready for a round of Q &A. She and Gina had a late check out, so she wouldn't have to rush after the conference closed. A card had been slipped under the door of the suite some time the night before. It was a note from Grayson letting her know that he would give her a call over the weekend and his email address. She had smiled at the thoughtfulness of it. The rose he had given her was now sitting on top of her suitcase.

As everyone took their seats, Janette noticed that there was someone still standing at the back of the room. She focused in as the moderators gave the audience instructions, and realized that it was Grayson. He gave her a deep smile, and a wave, and then backed out of the room with his suitcase. Janette didn't wave back, but gave him a smile as the moderator came over to hand her a mic.

ABOUT THE AUTHOR

DM Brockington is from the Lowcountry of South Carolina.

When she's not reading urban fantasy, paranormal, or contemporary fiction novels she's writing them.

She has more books than she has time to read, a love/hate relationship with Netflix (loves all the options, hates the inevitable time suck), and looks for story in everything.